The
DEVIL'S
WIFE

The
DEVIL'S
WIFE

USA TODAY BESTSELLING AUTHOR
GEMMA JAMES

ISBN-13: 978-1534869219
ISBN-10: 1534869212

Note To Readers

The Devil's Wife is a dark romance with a BDSM edge that does NOT conform to safe, sane, and consensual practices. Includes explicit content and subject matter that may offend some readers. Intended for mature audiences. Book three in the *Devil's Kiss* series.

PROLOGUE

Snip.

The first lock of hair drifted to the tile. I brought the scissors to the left side of my head. Tears rimmed my eyes, threatening to spill over.

Snip. Snip. Snip.

My bare breasts heaved, nipples puckered. I didn't want to be warm. Warmth let feeling in, and I was suddenly and amazingly numb. Besides, warmth deceived with its inherent comfort, and comfort didn't exist in my world—not when he wanted me on my knees. Not when he wanted a meek and pliable and *obedient* robot for a wife.

Snip. Snip. Snip.

The severed strands circled my feet, freeing my shoulders from the weight of the red hair he loved so much. I couldn't help but recognize the significance in this moment, the symbolism, and it terrified me. It was only hair, but this rebellious act would change the tenuous dynamic we'd settled into for the past year. This very moment was about to fracture our world and expose the guts of our lies.

Narrowing my brows in determination, I faced the reflection of the woman whose eyes lit up with something foreign. Something challenging.

Something he wouldn't like.

This strange woman from another time—before rules and rituals and Gage Fucking Channing—was reborn as she lifted the shears and cut off the last section of hair.

Movement in the mirror drew my attention. He stood in the open doorway behind me, his posture inflexible as always. My eyes swerved to his before dropping to the belt clasped in his determined fist.

I whirled, crossed my arms, and silently threw down a challenge. A belt wouldn't cut it this time. I knew it, and now he did too. No, on the eve of our first anniversary, Gage would have to do better than that.

1. THE SOUND OF SILENCE

One week earlier

I was late. Not in the oh-my-God-I'm-pregnant kind of way, but in the I'm-going-to-get-my-ass-punished-for-this kind of way. As I inserted the key with an unsteady hand, Eve squirmed at my side on the stoop.

"Mommy," she whined. "I gotta pee."

"Okay, just a sec."

Gage's car isn't in the driveway.

I kept repeating that phrase in my head, trying to calm my nerves, but that wouldn't happen until this stubborn door opened. As I cursed under my breath and jiggled the key, my heart thundered at the thought that he could pull into the driveway any second and realize I was fifteen minutes late. The lock clicked over, and I shoved the door so hard it banged against the wall.

"Hurry up and use the potty, baby. I need to start dinner."

Fifteen damn minutes.

If I didn't act fast, Gage would learn of my tardiness, and then he might take away the key to my car. Heck, that wasn't even my biggest problem at the moment. As I set my purse on the entryway table, a text notification sounded from my cell.

Almost like an omen reflecting my thoughts.

I pulled the phone out of my purse and read the message.

I just want to talk. Think about it, ok?

That was the problem. I was thinking about it. I'd thought of nothing else since I'd run into him at the hospital.

It's not a good idea, I replied.

Neither was marrying him.

Ouch. He sure wasn't holding back the punches. Gnawing on my lip, I fired off another text, doing my best to ignore the time as it ticked away.

That's exactly why it's not a good idea. I don't want to fight.

A car approached, the whine of the engine muffled through the door. I peeked through the small window in the foyer and slumped in relief. Just a neighbor. Another text sounded, making me jump.

I don't want to fight either, Kayla. I just want to talk.

My thumbs hovered over the screen, ready to type *no*. But somewhere between thought and action, the no became a yes.

Ok, tomorrow.

I took a deep breath. Oh my God. What was I doing? I honestly didn't know, yet my fingers tapped the screen, telling him when and where to meet me. Telling him not to text again. Because him texting was dangerous. No, it was just plain reckless. Gage searched my phone at random.

I deleted the messages, shrugged out of my coat, and hung it in the closet. As I headed into the kitchen, I told myself to calm down. Otherwise, Gage would take one look at me and know something was up.

My hands were still trembling as I turned on the oven and slid the casserole I'd prepared that morning onto the rack. Next, I worked to set the stage with a wine glass sitting on the breakfast bar, half full as if it had been there a while. Hopefully, Gage wouldn't take a sip because the Pinot Gris was too cold to have been poured fifteen minutes ago when I *should* have been home.

"I'm hungry," Eve said, appearing at my side as I fretted over the preheat beep going off.

Please go off before he gets home.

"Dinner will be ready soon. Did you put your things away?"

Eve nodded, pride in her eyes because she was a big girl now. "Can I watch TV?"

"Sure, but just until dinner."

Five minutes later, the oven sounded its preheated status, and Gage walked in. Sipping my wine, I relaxed my face into an expression of serenity, but my foot itched to tap against the leg of the bar stool.

"Sorry I'm late," he said, embracing me from behind. He looped an arm across my abdomen, turned my face toward his, and planted his mouth on mine. We might have kissed for an hour because I lost track of time as our tongues mated.

Sighing into his kiss, I brought my fingers to the spot below his ear and ran the length of his jaw, loving the prickle of his five o'clock shadow.

He drew back, leaving my head spinning from the intoxication that was purely him. "How was yoga today?" he asked.

"It was…" I blinked, recovering from his heated greeting. "Relaxing."

He nudged my neck with his nose. "Did you talk to any men today?"

"Of course not." Right then, I'd never been more grateful that he couldn't see my eyes and the lie in them.

"Good girl." He gingerly nibbled the side of my throat, right where my pulse throbbed.

"Hungry?" I asked, breathless.

"Mmm-hmm. Depends on what we're talking about."

Despite my frazzled nerves, I laughed. "Food, you pervert. Dinner will be ready soon."

Eve bounded into the kitchen, and Gage let me go so he could greet her. He swung her into his arms and asked her about her day.

"Ms. Sherman teached us the letter *M*," she said.

Gage glanced my way, debauchery in his eyes, and that intense stare stripped me of my defenses from across the kitchen. M for Master. We were both thinking it.

"It makes a sound like *moo*," she said with a giggle.

Gage set her back on her feet, laughing as he mussed her hair. "You're getting too smart for your britches, princess."

"Am I as smart as you now?"

"Way smarter than me."

She giggled again before racing out of the kitchen, her little feet pounding the hardwood.

He returned to me at the breakfast bar, and his hands landed on my shoulders, massaging some of the tension away, making me relax into him. Until he spoke. "I'm taking away your yoga privileges next week."

My eyes widened. "Why?"

"I have other plans for you."

Heartbeat rising to a furious staccato, I slid off the bar stool, needing distance. Some space to decipher what he was up to. "What kind of plans?"

"Guess you'll have to wait and see." His tone gave nothing away, and I had no idea if these *plans* were good or bad.

Having this discussion with him would be easier if I had a reason to keep my hands busy, my attention focused on something other than him. I crossed the kitchen and pulled salad makings from the fridge.

"Simone will be disappointed," I said, rinsing a tomato.

"Your friends have no bearing on my decisions, Kayla."

I bit my tongue. Last thing I wanted was to give him another reason to harp on my choice of friends. He didn't like her, and it had taken a lot of effort on my part to get him to allow our friendship. His high-handed attitude was starting to burrow into my skin a little more each day. I sliced into the tomato with extra oomph, slamming the knife onto the cutting board with a loud *chop*.

"I agreed to your yoga classes as long as you didn't forget your place." He leaned toward me, his long and slender fingers curling around the edge of the granite counter. Granite just like his expression. "Do you need a harsher reminder tonight?"

I dropped the knife and tried not to glower at him. "That isn't necessary."

"Glad to hear it." He picked up the discarded knife and took over, moving on to peel and chop a cucumber. "After next week, we'll revisit your yoga classes with Simone."

And right then I knew this wasn't about yoga at all. He didn't like Simone. Clearly, he was trying to put a wedge between our friendship.

"Gage, please. It's only twice a week."

"I don't care. I want you here and available. Can I trust you to obey me, or do I need to work from home next week to make sure you stay put?" His sideway glance tingled down my spine. I studied the profile of his gorgeous face, searching for signs that he *knew*.

"That was a question, Kayla."

I tamped down rising panic. "There's no need for you to do that. I'll talk to Simone and let her know I'm not free."

Damn it.

"Good, then it's settled."

Neither of us spoke until we sat down with Eve at the dinner table. Gage and Eve chatted easily like they always did, but my mind wandered to next week and my new dilemma.

"Are you excited about the slumber party next weekend?" Gage asked Eve.

I picked at the chicken broccoli casserole on my plate, my stomach twisting into knots over my half-discussion half-argument with him. Even worse, my lie ate away at me more than ever.

"Leah said it's a *pajama* party, Daddy."

Gage's sapphire eyes sparkled with meaning, not only because she'd called him Daddy—something she didn't do very often—but the slumber party was a reminder of our anniversary next weekend. Knowing Gage the way I did, I figured his plans included something equally diabolical and romantic.

After dinner, I cleared the table and gave Eve a bath. Our nightly routine of chores, bedtime stories, and at least five kisses and tuck-ins before she settled underneath her princess comforter passed quietly.

This was our life. We sat down for dinner every evening, and on Mondays we played board games as a family. Wednesdays were movie and popcorn night. Fridays…Fridays ended late, long after we said goodnight to Eve since Gage had decided a month ago that I needed a weekly session with his belt to remind me that I belonged to him. That Friday ritual had started after he'd given me access to my purse, keys, and phone. It had started after I'd begun using yoga classes as a cover.

Each week since, when the sharp bite of his belt flamed my ass, I fretted over the idea that he knew. Considering the tension between us tonight…I hated that today was Friday.

I switched off the lights in the kitchen, grabbed a raunchy romance from the bookshelf in the living room, and headed toward the hall. Gage had retreated to his office and would probably be in there for a while dealing with the pile of paperwork on his desk. I expected him to be at least an hour, giving me a short reprieve from his Friday ritual, so I was surprised to find him blocking my way to our bedroom. The novel slipped from my fingers.

We didn't need words as he took my hand and ushered me into our bedroom. The door shut with a soft click, followed by the turn of a lock. As he unbuckled his belt, I crossed to the bed and bent over the mattress.

I widened my stance, willing my four-inch stilettos to support me. Willing my legs to stop quivering. Silence blared through the room, a disquiet that brought the *thump-thump-thump* of blood rushing through my veins to the forefront, amplifying everything.

The chill in the room, drifting over my skin and causing gooseflesh. The slow and deliberate way he slid the belt from his pant loops. The soft but insistent pad of his shoes on the floor as he neared me.

Despite the phantom echo of pain roaring along my nerve endings, I'd never felt so sexy, bent over the way I was with my hair splayed on the mattress, one cheek pressed to the comforter. Vulnerable to his every whim.

I gripped the hem of my skirt and waited for his command. Seconds ticked by until a full minute passed. I bit my lip to keep from squirming, to remain quiet as he expected. I knew he waited behind me with that strap of leather looped in his fist. This preamble was part of the thrill for him, part of the ritual. He enjoyed making me wait with my breath suspended. Fear crept in during this time like it had last week and the week before. Fear that he knew, and this was his way of punishing me for it.

"Lift your skirt."

Pound. Pound. Pound.

How could he not hear my heartbeat? It throbbed in my ears as I pulled up my skirt, sliding the silky material over an ass left bare for his pleasure.

Always bare. Always ready for him.

I sucked in a breath, let it shudder out, and gripped my skirt so tightly my fingers ached. We entered another unbearable period of waiting, and I shook with knowing that when his belt did strike my ass for the first time, it would come as a surprise.

Like the week before, and the week before that.

That first lash would steal my breath and make my eyes burn, would cramp my legs and—

Thwack!

I opened my mouth, but no sound came out.

"One," he said because I wasn't allowed to speak during these weekly *reminders.*

I blinked several times to hold back tears, and my deception wrapped around my throat, cinching until it nearly choked me. Another lick of fire streaked across my ass, followed by his hoarse voice.

"Two."

Eighteen more to go.

The strikes were few compared to his usual allotment,

but they were three times the strength. On number eleven, I almost pleaded for him to stop. But like the week before, and the week before that, I pressed my lips together and endured the next one in quiet anguish.

It wasn't so much that it hurt. Wasn't that it was degrading. This new ritual of his was…

Confusing.

And if I spoke and fractured our unspoken code of silence, I was scared of what would come out. Would I show my weakness by begging and crying? Would I confess? Would he utter the words I dreaded most?

I know your secret.

I didn't want to find out, so I took the beating. Week after week, our ritual settled into something that just was, something that transpired between Master and slave in unnerving silence.

"Twenty."

Finality rang in my ears, bounced around my mind. His belt clattered to the floor, and the sound of his zipper stabbed at my control, primed me to tremble under the firm pressure of his palms on my stinging ass.

I wanted to moan.

I wanted to push my ass toward him in invitation.

God, I *wanted*.

And he knew it, tortured me with it, had me wrapped long before his cock nudged the center of my depravity. My breath hitched, stalling in my lungs until the edges of my vision grew fuzzy.

Until my world narrowed only to him.

To him dangling me over the precipice with his strong

hands gripping my hips, holding me in place as he rocked into me. To the stillness of our interlocked bodies and the rush of adrenaline begging me to move against him. Begging me to beg him.

But I understood without him saying a word. I was to have no control. He didn't permit me to take pleasure, nor to voice my distress in having to hold back. And God, it was torture not to grind against him, to moan and plead for more as he began to thrust.

Finally, he slammed into me the way I needed him to.

Then he did it again.

Deeper.

So rough and brutal and animalistic that the power of his cock drove me to my toes, pushing me higher onto the mattress until my back arched under the onslaught. He grunted while I sucked in quick, shallow breaths as our bodies slapped together.

I balled my hands around my skirt, squeezed my eyes shut, and tried to block my impending orgasm. And I would. I'd do whatever it took to hold back. I gnawed on my lip, bit down on the comforter, ground my fists into my sides. Desperation threatened to swallow me whole. Desperation appealed to the pressure building, whispering to *just let go.*

But I couldn't. I'd broken my oath to obey enough already, and I'd atone for it. If—*when*—he learned of my deceit, I'd pay dearly. But stopping the eruption seemed damn near impossible.

Don't come.

In my mind, I visualized a cage where I locked away

my free-fall into ecstasy, but my pussy tightened around him anyway, becoming slicker. Needier. Greedy.

Shit, he felt good. Not even my burning ass overshadowed the way in which he claimed me.

With a strangled groan, he lifted me onto the mattress, spread my knees, and shoved me to my elbows before plunging deep—so deep that the base of his cock stretched me wide. He tugged on my hair, yanking my head back, and the smack of his balls on my clit almost sent me over the edge.

I will not come.

Not until he uttered the word. And he would, soon. Because he was close.

Just a little bit long—

"Come."

A muted scream tore from my gaping mouth, and I did the only thing I could. I obeyed.

2. TREACHEROUS

I often asked myself why I'd married Gage. He wasn't the easiest to love, and he wasn't the easiest man to live with. But on those dark days when his intensity became too much to bear, all I had to do was watch him with my daughter.

The following morning, I stood to the side of the dining room entrance and did just that. Pushing my bangs from my eyes, I saw him turn her pancake into a smiley face. He loved her, but more importantly, she loved him.

He'd not only kept my baby girl alive by bringing her back from the brink of death, but he'd given her something I feared she'd never have. He'd given her a father. So during those times when I hung from the ceiling, my toes barely touching the ground, and endured the bite of his belt, I remembered.

I remembered on days when the belt wasn't enough, and he moved on to harsher toys. The paddle riddled with holes. The riding crop that induced a mystical sensation between my thighs—a feeling I couldn't discern from sexual hunger. And the deceptive flogger with its soft strips of leather. That thing inflicted more pain than his belt if he put enough strength behind the lashes.

But paddles and floggers were child's play to Gage. He reserved the truly horrific implements for severe infractions despite them being hard limits. Every time my gaze crossed paths with the bullwhip in the basement, a knife ripped through my chest. That symbol of agony bled memories from its coiled place on the wall. I couldn't help but cower at the sight because I knew I wouldn't escape it forever.

He'd promised a caning if I left the house without permission.

He'd promised to gag me if I lied to him.

He'd promised a date with the bullwhip if I spoke to his brother again.

I was three for three.

"Mommy!" Eve's smile, along with the sweet scent of pancakes, pulled me into the dining room. As I greeted her, I spied the upward curve of Gage's lips. He loved making her happy. I was certain the few times he'd scolded her for stepping out of line had upset him more than it had her.

I would have never guessed a man as complex, sadistic, and controlling as Gage could harbor such a soft spot for a child. Perhaps that hint of vulnerability in him, that glimpse of kindness he rarely displayed, was the reason he'd captured my heart a year ago when I agreed to marry him. If I were truthful though, I'd hurtled headfirst into loving him before then, and it hadn't mattered if my sanity shattered upon the fall.

"Gage made me the smiley face again. Do you want one too?"

"I'd love one," I said with a shaky smile as I slid into a seat. I wanted to share her enthusiasm, her perspective on life, seen through the veil of innocence. But for me, enthusiasm was only found in the bedroom, and I'd lost my innocence long before Gage had gotten his hands on me.

Somehow, that quiet acknowledgment made what I planned to do today a little easier, made the guilt a little more bearable. I liked to think I was an honest person, someone with a healthy moral compass, but I was far from a saint. I'd crossed that line the day I'd stolen ten grand from Gage to save Eve.

And I'd do it again without hesitation or remorse.

Eve shoved a huge bite of pancake into her mouth and dripped syrup onto her nightgown. She didn't seem to care, and neither did Gage, even though some of the sticky goo dropped onto the dining table, which would surprise most people if they didn't look beyond the carefully groomed man in the expensive suits. Something could be said about a man who didn't mind the sticky fingers of a six-year-old.

Gage set a plate in front of me, squirted a smiley face made of whipped cream onto the perfectly golden pancake, and then he bent and pressed his mouth to mine. It wasn't a passionate kiss. We didn't even part our lips. But the way he brought his hand to my cheek and feathered his fingers over my suddenly flushed skin melted my heart.

Eve giggled and said something about kissing and a tree, but I was too breathless and flustered to hear if she'd recited the ageless rhyme correctly.

He drifted to my ear and imparted a whispered, "Good morning, beautiful."

He made me feel beautiful, and that only added to my treachery because I'd dressed with someone else in mind.

"Morning," I said, sidestepping my guilt as I cut my pancake into neat little sections. "I forgot to pick up the dry cleaning yesterday. They close early today, so I thought I'd take care of that after breakfast." Willing my face to give nothing away, I met his eyes and silently asked for his permission.

We had a system in place to protect Eve from our alternative lifestyle, an unspoken code of rules and protocols. If the answer was yes, he'd give the go ahead, but if I wasn't allowed to leave the house, he'd tell me not to worry about it today.

I held my breath and waited. Not only would I get a spanking for my failure to do the chore, but I'd "forgotten" on purpose so I'd have an excuse to leave the house. Deep down, I'd known I'd go, regardless of what I said in my texts yesterday. Even so, I'd deliberated too long over stopping by the cleaners, and the consequence had been coming home late.

A close call, and all because I couldn't help but flirt with disaster. Flirt with the forbidden.

I continued to hold his gaze, praying he wouldn't read the subterfuge in my expression, the stress threatening to pull at the corners of my mouth.

Finally, he gave a slight nod. "I need to speak to you before you go."

"Okay," I said, hoping my relief wasn't too apparent. Showing signs of relief upon confirmation of an impending punishment wasn't a typical reaction. He made it hurt when he spanked me for an infraction, and if I got wet, he used the nipple clamps and started over.

After breakfast, Gage loaded the dishwasher while I settled Eve in her bedroom with her collection of Barbies. While she quietly played, lost in her own realm of pretend, I waited with my stomach in knots.

Gage stepped into view, and one glance at his firm mouth commanded me to my feet. I bent and placed a kiss on the crown of Eve's head. "Be good, baby. I need to run an errand. I won't be long, okay?"

"'Kay." She was too wrapped up in her dolls to notice me leaving. I quietly shut the door before following Gage down the hall to our bedroom. He'd had the room soundproofed after we'd married. Neither of us wanted Eve to hear our loud cries of ecstasy. Or my howls of pain.

He didn't punish me often in this room—usually only when Eve was home, and we needed an accessible space where we could still be close in case she needed us.

Gage turned down the child monitor, and Eve's soft voice faded to a static whisper. He sank into the designated spanking chair, but I stalled in the middle of the room.

I fucking hated this.

I loved the kinky play between the sheets, even the more brutal sessions with his various toys in the basement because he usually mixed pain with pleasure. But the punishments...they were bullshit. I thought I could tolerate his never-ending need to control me, but I had to admit, if only to myself, that these past few weeks of stolen freedom had opened my eyes to how he'd isolated me inside his vortex of sex, dominance, and sadism.

Why couldn't I have the good without the bad? Did I not deserve that? More importantly, why did he need to hurt me? To punish me. I'd turned this puzzle over in my head too many times to count. I figured it stemmed from losing Liz. His world had cracked and fissured under him, and that single, irrevocable moment had forever changed him.

Part of me wondered if this was his way of punishing her for her affair with Ian. Was he unconsciously using me as a proxy?

"Look at me."

My gaze snapped to his, and only then did I realize I'd been staring at his feet. I loved him in pajama pants, his feet bare, hair mussed. God, he was sexy as hell, more sinful than the devil himself because he appeared more human that way. Less intimidating.

"You know the rules, so quit stalling."

I wanted to argue with him, but that never ended well. In fact, it ended with an extended date with his firm hand, and I didn't have time for that today. The sooner I gave him what he wanted, the sooner he'd give me what I wanted.

The freedom to walk out the front door.

I trudged across the room and let him pull me over his knee. He lifted my skirt, using his usual method of slow torture. It shouldn't take thirty seconds to bare my ass, but he managed to draw it out that long.

"Do you have anything you'd like to tell me, Kayla?"

"I forgot to pick up the dry cleaning yesterday. I need to be punished."

He gripped my hair and tugged. "Who am I?"

"My Master."

"I will always be your Master, but apparently you've forgotten lately."

The title had never settled on my tongue with ease, but in certain situations, he wouldn't let me get away with calling him anything else. I'd learned when to choose my battles, and calling him Master wasn't one I intended to fight.

He settled me against his abs, tucking me in with a strong arm and leaving his right hand free to deliver the punishing strikes. "Your disobedience needs to stop."

"I'm sorry, Master."

"Apology isn't enough. You're going to beg me for each swat."

I gritted my teeth. He was infuriating! His rituals and rules and consequences for the slightest offenses…they were too much. They were downright absurd. But I had no one to blame but myself. He'd shown his true colors from day one—that day in his office when he'd used Eve's cancer to blackmail me into sexual submission.

Shameless and without remorse, he'd forced my legs

apart and fingered me while my coworkers went about their business like any other day. But my entire life had changed in that fifteen minutes. I'd signed the contract on his terms and promptly fell down the rabbit hole.

Fell into an addiction named Gage Channing, and not even putting a year between us and running half way across the country had stopped him in the end.

"Beg," he said.

"Please spank me."

"I'm not convinced. Convince me, Kayla. Tell your Master how badly you deserve to be punished."

"I need to be punished. Please, Master. Spank me."

"No." He pulled me flush against his hard body. "Explain to me why I should give you my hand."

"Because I forgot to pick up the dry cleaning?" A note of question entered my tone.

"That's part of it, but I think you know the real reason."

He knows! Shit, he knows.

Icy dread sludged through me. I hoped he didn't notice the shudder in my bones. How I managed to keep my voice steady remained a mystery.

"I don't know what you're talking about. If you tell me, then I can beg you for what I deserve."

"You've been absent from this relationship lately. I don't know where your mind is, but it's not on how to serve and please me. Remind me again what your job is."

"To serve, please, and obey my Master." I recited the oath with such precision it fell flat to my ears.

He didn't seem to hear the lack of truth in those

words. "And what is my responsibility to you, baby?"

"To love and care for me."

"Have I not done those things?"

"You have."

"Then I won't ask again. Beg me to make your ass red, and mean it."

I closed my eyes and uttered the words, swallowed the self-disgust in my throat. His hand came down with too little force but with obvious intent. The easier he went on me, the faster I'd get wet.

And he never passed up an opportunity to clamp my nipples.

I willed my body to behave and waited for the next swat, but it never came. Silence ticked by, ringing in my ears, increasing the speed of my pulse. What was he waiting for…?

Oh.

"Please, Master. Again."

"Should I go easy on you?"

"No, Master."

"Why not?"

"It pleases you to hurt me." It was true enough, and if he stopped playing with me and just fucking struck me with a punishing hand, maybe I could control myself. "Please, Master. Spank me hard."

He complied, and I asked for another. I asked for so many that I lost count. When would it be enough for him?

"Please…" My voice trailed off, and I resisted squirming on his lap as my ass blazed. I didn't want to push him and prolong the punishment. I'd learned to accept his sadism, his need to mark me as his for the smallest of reasons. Life was easier when I gave in.

"Please, what?"

Please stop.

"Please spank me again, Master."

His hand came down with a loud smack.

Harder.

Faster.

He was escalating from punishing to vicious. I couldn't contain my strangled cries after a while. I'd never been more appreciative of the soundproofed room. Last thing I wanted was for Eve to hear me.

"Please!" I yelped, then forced a plea for more between tight lips.

"More, you'll get. My hand loves your ass. I have all day." Each time he hit me, I jerked atop his lap, blinked through the burning tears pooling in my eyes. But on some masochistic level, I knew I deserved every strike of his hand.

A desolate tear fell to the floor, and I fell silent for too long.

"Do you think you've been punished enough?"

I thought long and hard about my answer, but there was no right one because either option could potentially land me in his lap for another twenty minutes...or longer. "Yes, Master. I won't forget the dry cleaning again."

"Are you wet?"

"No, Master."

But it wouldn't take much to get me there. I stood,

facing away, and bent so he could complete the punishment by *checking* me. It was a degrading thing to do —bending over, fingers grasping my ankles so he could probe my sex for signs of forbidden arousal. At the first touch of his fingers spreading me open, seeking my hot center, I bit my lip hard.

"Spread your legs."

I did so, and he pushed his fingers so deep, I was sure the full length of them laid claim to my treacherous cunt. The needy thing was a cunt. It didn't know when to fucking behave, and I was a stroke away from creaming all over his hand. I counted the various lines in the hardwood, watched the way my hair gently swished the floor. And I thought of the front door and how I needed to be going through it *now*.

That wouldn't happen if I let my body betray me. Again. I should have more self-restraint by now. How many times had he tormented me with denial? With orgasm control? He'd trained me so well that I rarely came unless he commanded me to. But controlling my body on the cusp of a punishment, no matter how degrading or hurtful, was torturous, and he knew it.

"Good girl," he murmured, slowly withdrawing his fingers from me. I rose to an upright position. But he wasn't through with me; he spun me around and pulled me onto his lap.

"You did well, baby." He caught my mouth, drawing me into a kiss that made my muscles tense and freeze. A kiss that torpedoed through me and did what his punishment hadn't; turned me to liquid fire. Unfurled me into abandon. Obliterated my mind because I couldn't think beyond his tongue sliding against mine.

His cock grew heavy between my legs, and I fell victim to need. I was free of thought, doubt, or regret as I pushed against his hard shaft, tainting his pajama bottoms with my arousal and wishing like hell the flannel wasn't between us.

He broke our fevered connection and inched back, pinning me with hooded indigo eyes. "Do you deserve to be fucked?"

I almost said yes, but the gleam in his gaze bespoke of sadistic fuckery. It was a trick question. "No, Master."

"Good answer." Gently, he untangled my quaking body from his and pushed me to the floor between his spread knees. I must have fallen under some devious spell because I couldn't tear my eyes away as he tugged his pants down and freed his erection.

Adrenaline rushed my veins, heat erupted at my core, and I licked my lips, already tasting him on my tongue. Already hearing the way he groaned low in his throat whenever I teased the head of his gorgeous cock.

Imagined him surrendering to me, if only for a few minutes.

"You want me in your mouth?"

"Yes, Master."

"That's too bad." He folded his fingers around his shaft and stroked the length. Up. Down. Slower than slow. "You don't deserve to suck my cock."

My breath hitched, but I bit my tongue to keep from arguing with him.

"Open your mouth." He began pumping his smooth shaft. "Now, Kayla. *Open* your mouth."

I did as told and waited with parted lips. A few more strokes of his hand was all it took. Striking my ass had been all the foreplay he needed. Letting out a deep cry, he jumped to his feet, height towering over me, and squirted his release onto my face. I wiped his cum from my eyes and swallowed what had landed on my tongue.

A few heavy seconds passed. For some reason, he avoided my gaze. And that's when I realized it. When *he* realized it. Mutual understanding flowed between us. I needed freedom, and he needed absolute control. But which one of us would fold first? The foundation of our marriage had shifted, had been shifting for a while, and I suspected neither of us had acknowledged it until now.

He broke the silence. "Freshen up and take care of your errand." He offered his hand—an act of kindness, or a trap? Cautiously, I fit my hand into his and allowed him to haul me to my feet. But when I tried to move past him toward the bathroom, he halted me with a harsh grip on my chin, his thumb and forefinger pressing into his cum on my face.

"I want you back here by noon and not a minute later. Do you understand me?"

"Yes, Master."

He dropped his fingers to my collarbone, caressing the infinity collar that trapped my neck—the symbol that enslaved me under his ownership until the day I died... and maybe not even then.

"I don't enjoy being harsh with you. You probably

don't believe that, but it's true."

He was right. I didn't believe him. His sadism often did the driving. Gage was just a passenger to its depraved needs.

"But I know something is going on with you," he said. "Don't keep shit from me. Dishonesty will get you nowhere." He let me go, but his warning had the desired effect because I was shaking by the time I found sanctuary in the bathroom.

3. CLANDESTINE

A constant mist dampened my hair and coat. I preferred rain, as it dropped from the sky without giving the hope of leaving you dry. Mist was a creeper—you didn't realize you were soaked until it was too late. I feared what was how this meeting with Ian would go.

I can't believe I'm doing this.

But in the most secretive corners of my being, I'd known an eventual confrontation of some sort was on the horizon. It was only logical since he was Gage's brother. And I knew Ian well enough to know that he wouldn't settle for the way things had ended. The day we parted ways had haunted me for a while, as if we'd left something important unsaid, left a window open that needed closing.

Maybe that's what drew me to volunteer at the hospital in the first place. The idea that I'd bump into him…eventually. That I'd get the chance to do what I'd failed to do that day in the hospital after losing my baby. Make things right.

Was that even possible?

I was about to find out. As I entered the coffee shop next to the cleaners, flutters of anticipation took flight in my stomach. The door swished closed behind me. Wiping the moisture from my temples, I scanned the space for him, my gaze falling on several men with dark hair before I found Ian.

He sat by himself at a small table at the far end of the shop, and something about his demeanor bothered me. Made me consider him in a different light. He wore his hair in a buzz cut, much shorter than I ever remembered, and his clothes were unusually rumpled. He seemed distracted as I approached—preoccupied as he stirred a spoon in his coffee. One brown loafer tapped the floor, and he gazed out the window, failing to notice my presence.

I almost turned and fled. Meeting him was wrong, unfair to both him and Gage. But…I had to see him. My selfishness disgusted me, and suddenly I was grateful Gage had whaled on my ass that morning.

Drawing a fortifying breath, I gathered the last threads of my resolve and slid into the seat across from him. His attention broke away from the fascinating show of birds flocking through the trees lining the street.

"I wasn't sure you'd come." His gaze dropped to my modest cleavage for a moment, then his eyes settled on my face again.

"I wasn't sure I'd come either." A lie. The instant the elevator at the hospital yesterday had confined us for the duration of seven floors, I'd known this was the moment

I'd been waiting for. The moment I'd been dreading.

My opportunity to play with fire.

He leaned forward, and his hazel eyes imparted an intensity that almost matched Gage's. I could detect the relation so easily now. I wasn't sure how I'd missed it before. They both commanded with their presence, though Ian did it in a quiet, unthreatening way compared to his brother. Suddenly, I wondered if that made him more dangerous.

A creeper mist waiting to drench me.

"You look good, Kayla."

The way he said my name sent a sharp ping through my heart—not big enough to be a knife, but not small enough to be a harmless pinprick either. I'd missed him this past year, but I couldn't voice it. I could barely admit it to myself.

"I probably shouldn't have come."

"Does Gage know you're here?"

My first instinct was to lie. Ian wouldn't like the answer, and I didn't have the energy to defend my marriage to him. Before I could answer, he scowled, indicating I was as translucent as sheer silk.

"Is he going to beat you for seeing me?"

"No." Even as I spoke, I knew there was more deceit than truth in the denial. When it came to Ian, Gage would blow a gasket in a heartbeat. "He's been seeing a counselor."

"Still making excuses."

"I'm not making excuses." No. I was flat-out lying to myself. Now it was my turn to watch the birds zipping through the mist outside, their wings fluttering.

"So this won't bother him? You and me," he said, gesturing to the space between us, "sitting in a crowded coffee shop, simply *talking*?"

It would definitely bother him. More than bother him. Even worse, it bothered me because I had no business being here. But a force I couldn't fight had propelled me to volunteer at his place of employment—essentially putting myself in his path. Now I sat across from him, an arm's length away from the one man on this planet I was forbidden to think about, let alone talk to.

My web of lies had me teetering on a slippery slope.

"I'll take your silence as a yes," he mumbled.

"You're right. He wouldn't like it." No doubt about it. Gage would feel betrayed, flayed to the bone. For someone as strong and dominant as Gage, he wounded easier than most people.

Ian raised a brow. "Why did you agree to meet me then?"

I stared down at my hands. "I'm not sure."

"Maybe your subconscious is trying to tell you something."

I risked a peek at him. "What do you think it's trying to tell me?"

"That you married the wrong man."

That was bold, even for Ian. "I don't regret marrying him."

He grabbed my hand. "Then *why* are you here, Kayla?" He thumbed the ring on my finger, but his quizzical gaze remained fixed on me.

I pulled my hand back and stood, and the chair scraped across the floor with an earsplitting screech. "Why are you here?" I tossed his words back into his face with a glare. "It's been a whole fucking year, Ian. Why now?"

"Sit down."

His tone was too similar to Gage's. Too commanding. That was the only reason I sank into my seat again. Habit. Gage had trained me well, though bending to another man's commands wasn't the result he'd aimed for. I tried not to fidget in my seat, especially when Ian leaned toward me again.

"Do you believe in fate?" he asked.

That was a difficult question. If I said yes, then did that mean Gage blackmailing me had been fate's doing? "I don't know."

"Well I believe in fate. Running into you yesterday was a sign." He took my hand again, refusing to let go this time. "I hear you've been volunteering in the children's wing. Is that true?"

I nodded as acid rose in my throat.

"What prompted you to do that?"

"I don't know," I whispered.

"You don't know much of anything, do you? Do you even know why you married him?"

"I'm not talking to you about this. I shouldn't have come." I tried removing myself from his grasp, but he held steady.

"He's got that much power over you?" he asked, incredulous. "He fucks you a few times and you're hooked. Unbelievable."

My heart sank. Apparently not even a year of distance had lessened his bitterness. "My marriage is none of your business. You have no idea what you're talking about." What he didn't understand was that Gage had power because I gave it to him. I gave him control. I willingly called him Master, gave him my body freely. I allowed him to hurt me when and how he liked. I followed his strict rules, wore toe crushing stilettos daily because he wanted me to. I bent, and bent, and bent some more because I got off on the obsession. No man would ever love me as fiercely and possessively as Gage Channing.

Yet I missed being *me*, the old me...the me who didn't have to ask for permission to do something as simple as pick up the fucking dry cleaning. The me who, despite a year of not seeing Ian, refused to stop caring about him in some small corner of my heart.

This day—the day I'd irrevocably stepped out of line —could be the day that brought everything crashing to the ground.

"Fine, Kayla. Your marriage to him is none of my business. But the fact that you're sitting across from me now, barely able to look me in the eye, is my business."

"This was a mistake," I said, finally extricating myself from his hold. Ian and I had too much history for this to feel so awkward. Yet it did, and it was my fault because I had no valid reason for meeting him. A year ago, I'd chosen his brother over him. Nothing had changed since then. Gage was still my husband. Still the man who owned me, whether I wanted him to or not. The man I loved, whether I wanted to or not.

"You've made plenty of mistakes," he said. "What's one more?"

My breath caught in my throat, and I couldn't hide the surprise in my expression. "What do you want from me?"

"I want to see you again. Meet me in my office on Monday? I've got a short shift, so I'm free around noon."

"I can't do that."

"Yes, you can. I talked to your boss. She already told me you volunteer on Mondays."

"What do you think is going to happen between us?" I held my breath, afraid of his answer.

"Nothing, unless you want something to happen."

I jumped to my feet. "I need to get home." My voice came out a strangled mess, revealing too much. The pain that fisted my heart. Would I ever be able to look at him and not want to crack in two?

He rose, slowly rounded the table, and before I could process what was about to happen, it happened. He pulled me into his arms, held on tight, and buried his face in my hair. I went stiff in his embrace, knowing that I was on shaky ground. Knowing that letting him touch me was the worst idea ever. But as the seconds ticked by, I couldn't help but relax into him. I was weak. Needy. I needed this.

Because Gage never *just* held me. He made me feel a spectrum of emotions, from fiery passion to lust to rage to suffocating possession, but he refused to show vulnerability. The part of him I loved the most—the man with a heart made of more than just ice—was barely around anymore.

And I missed that man so fucking much.

"I took so much for granted," Ian said, his tone thick with regret. His fingers tangled in my hair, and he tilted my head back. "I'll never make that mistake with you again."

I freed myself from his tempting arms and put some much-needed space between us. I'd made a massive mistake by meeting him today. The realization clenched my insides, and I felt on the verge of throwing up.

If Gage ever found out, not only would he be livid, but this would hurt him.

"I have to go." I pivoted and strode toward the front of the cafe without looking back, and I prayed to whoever was listening that I'd have enough time to pick up the dry cleaning and make it home by noon.

4. CONTROL

I arrived home with two minutes to spare. The house was too silent, giving off a vibe of abandonment. Too quiet because my daughter and Gage were nowhere to be found. The living room and kitchen were empty. I checked Gage's office before peeking inside Eve's room, but they were vacant as well.

Trepidation clutched my gut as I halted outside our bedroom. I knew he was home—I'd spied his car in the driveway. I could practically feel him beyond our bedroom door. Pushing it open, I wasn't surprised to find him waiting in the spanking chair. His guarded expression made me nervous. I couldn't read him, and I hated his cool and collected mask more than anything.

"Where's Eve?" I asked, clutching the dry cleaning in my hands.

"Leah's mother picked her up. She's spending the day with them."

Alarm bells rang in my head. "You didn't discuss it with me first?" I tried to keep my voice level, but in the back of my mind, I worried that he'd had me followed, was terrified he'd seen me in Ian's arms. This morning had convinced me that he knew *something* was up, but if he figured out I'd met with his brother…

I tried not to shrink at the thought.

"Who's in charge in this marriage, Kayla?" He rose, took the dry cleaning from me, and placed it on the bed. His expectant gaze settled on my face, and I realized it wasn't a rhetorical question.

"You are."

He nodded. "I'm not just your husband. I'm your Master. I don't discuss things with you."

"When it comes to me, maybe, but she's my daughter. You can't—"

He pressed a finger to my lips. "You should quit while you're ahead." I ceased arguing, and he dropped his hand. "Prepare for me in the basement."

"Am I in trouble?" I asked, anxiety thundering in my chest.

He knows. God, he knows.

The severity of his expression softened. "No, baby." He stroked my cheek with the back of his hand. "You're not in trouble."

I let out a small breath of relief, hopefully inconsequential enough that he wouldn't notice. But if he didn't intend to punish me, then that could only mean one thing.

"So today is about play?"

He gripped my jaw between his forefinger and thumb. "I know it's been a few days since I've had you on your knees properly, but that doesn't excuse you." His firm hold wasn't designed to inflict pain—he only did it to emphasize that he held all the power. "How do you address me?"

"I'm sorry, Master."

"No need for an apology. Just be a good little slave for your Master and do as you're told." One corner of his mouth quirked up. "You might like what I have in store for you. Or not, depending on how you look at it."

My heartbeat took off without me. God, how could he still make me this nervous? I'd lived with him for a year—a whole damn year—but the problem wasn't familiarity. The problem was the exact opposite; I knew him *too* well…which meant I knew better than to guess at what was coming next because Gage was as volatile as he was sexy.

"Don't take too long. I'll be down shortly." He brushed his lips over mine before disappearing through the doorway.

I made my way to the basement's entrance, found the key in its hiding place above the door—out of Eve's reach—and ventured inside. The temperature dropped, and the air grew chillier as I descended the stairs. He liked the way the cold hardened my nipples, so I didn't dare turn up the thermostat.

I eyed the floor where he expected to find me, naked and kneeling. Waiting. Even though I didn't have much time, I wandered into the bathroom and finger-combed my deep red locks. The distressed expression of the woman in the mirror gave me pause. Uncertainty strained her features, but her cheeks were also flushed from the exhilaration of the unknown.

My fingers caught in a stubborn tangle, and I nearly growled because I didn't have a say in how I wore my hair. It had grown too long, too heavy, and I was tempted to cut it despite Gage's orders that I leave it be. He liked to yanked on it during sex, so I wasn't allowed to come near it with scissors. But it was *my* hair, and I was the one who had to comb through the knots every day.

Expelling a weary sigh, I removed my blouse and exposed my breasts, shoved my skirt down my legs until it bunched around my feet. Save for the infinity collar that never left my neck, I stood in the bathroom, unclothed and shivering. Unless I wanted play to turn into punishment, I'd better quit stalling and get into position.

He entered a few minutes later, his shirt and shoes gone. The tailor made slacks he favored hugged him in all the right places, showcasing the huge erection straining beneath his zipper. I knelt on the hard floor with my thighs spread just how he liked, hands clasped at the small of my back, eyes downcast. I thrust my breasts upward to offer him the best view of my nipples.

"Good girl."

Why his approval traveled through my system, heating the core of what made me a woman, I'd never understand. I'd stopped agonizing over the whys of our relationship dynamics a long time ago. We were what we were. I was who I was. No point in fighting it just because what we had wasn't conventional. It just *was*.

He neared me with purpose, unbuttoning his pants,

pulling his zipper down. With confident hands, he took his cock out and folded his fingers around the base. He didn't have to command me—simply standing before me with his erection aimed at my mouth was enough. I knew my place, anticipated his needs so well that pleasing him became the fuel for my hunger. It was second nature.

Keeping my hands clasped at my back, I leaned forward and ran my tongue along the underside of his cock. The tiny breath he took, sucked in between clenched teeth, was my reward. I softened my lips and pressed a kiss on his tip. His arousal moistened my lips, teased my tongue with the salty taste of him.

He groaned, his fingers sifting through my hair, holding me to him with a tender, hypnotic caress as he pushed into my mouth, shoving deep so I had no choice but to take his entire length.

He moaned as he plundered, his hips swiveling with each thrust, his cock as forceful as it was merciful. The need in him took over, and his pace increased. Breathing escalated—his and mine.

Shit, he was in a weird mood. Gage either fucked me hard, regardless of what hole he was using, or he just... loved me. Something about this felt in-between, on the edge of a brutal mouth fuck. Yet I sensed his restraint, and it confused the heck out of me.

"Kayla—" He halted with a gasp, his cock throbbing on my tongue, the head finding respite between my tonsils. My gag reflex kicked in, spasmed around his shaft.

He breathed in ragged bursts. "You know what gagging does to me."

I did, and I was bewildered because he held back instead of shoving deeper. I lifted my eyes, and I would have gladly knelt at his feet all day, his cock taking residence between my lips, if he'd look at me like that forever. With heated, indigo eyes that imparted his obsession in waves of longing, lust, and possessive madness.

I yearned for all of those things—yearned for our bodies twisted in the sheets, slick with the kind of sweat only mind-blowing sex could inspire. And I ached. Hell, how I ached and craved and thirsted for his weight on me, for his fists pinning my wrists to the bed. Taking what was his.

Leaving me helpless to stop it.

A shiver traveled through me. I whimpered, resisting the urge to touch myself, and silently begged him with my gaze.

He gritted his teeth. "You're not coming."

My heart sank, and I slammed back to reality with a harsh jolt. What if he'd found out about my clandestine meeting with Ian? What if this was all a sick and twisted game, and I'd be better off coming clean? With my mouth full of cock, I couldn't even do that.

"Don't give me that look. You always think the worst of me. Stop thinking you're being punished because you're not. *I'm* not coming either." He closed his eyes for a few moments and just breathed, as if he couldn't fathom not climaxing down my throat.

I couldn't fathom it either.

"Baby…" His eyes popped open, and he inhaled,

exhaled. "We're not coming until we celebrate the day I got your stubborn, sexy ass down the aisle." Letting out a furious groan of frustration, he pulled out then helped me to my feet.

"I don't understand," I said. "What are we doing down here then?"

Hauling me into his arms, he attacked my mouth as he carried me across the room. We all but fell into the St. Andrew's cross, his hands supporting my ass as my legs wrapped around his waist, our tongues clashing in battle. In the space of a few minutes, the basement had gone from freezing to an inferno. Perspiration crawled between my cleavage, bathing my skin in a sheen of pure lust.

We broke apart, and our eyes met and held.

"What we're doing down here," he began, nipping my bottom lip, "is beginning a torturous week of teasing." Another nibble, and then he whispered, "Practicing restraint through denial." He tempted the seam of my mouth with his tongue, and I parted my lips, inviting him inside again. "Practicing the art of edging."

Inch by agonizing inch, he pushed his cock into me, right to the hilt, and pinned my back to the wall with nothing more than his strong body.

"Arms up," he said.

I lifted my hands, already reaching for the chains meant to shackle me.

"You feel so damn good." His groan of self-control vibrated against my lips. He fumbled with the chains for a few moments, too caught up in the blaze roaring between us. Finally, he locked the cuff around my left wrist. "Too fucking good."

"So do you," I whispered, trembling as he pulsed inside me. "I need more."

"Who am I?"

"My Master." I gave him the title without hesitation. Would have given anything to feel him move.

He worked on securing my right wrist, and soon I hung from the cross, held up by nothing more than my wrists and the power in his thighs, the force of his cock.

"Tell your Master what you want."

"I want you to fuck me." Except I didn't. I wanted more. I wanted his body wrapped around mine, his arms caging me within his warmth and protection.

I wanted his love.

I hungered for the last decaying brick of his fortress to crumble, because even after being his wife for a year, he still hid parts of himself from me. Parts of himself I feared he'd never uncloak. It was easier to command me, to have me on my knees with his cock in my mouth, or bent over our mattress while he beat and fucked me than to expose the tatters of his soul.

"I'll fuck you," he said, thrusting in a slow, sadistic way designed to make me his. To keep me at his feet, underneath him, against the wall. "But sliding in and out of your sweet cunt won't end in orgasm for either of us. Think beyond sex. If you could have anything, what would it be?"

"To not be helpless." Once the words were out, settling between us, there was no taking them back.

He glanced at my outstretched arms. "Yet here you

are, your cunt begging to cream on my cock." He withdrew then dived in with a brutal thrust. A cry tore from my lips, part pain, part ecstasy.

"What do you want, Kayla?"

"Your submission." I felt my eyes go wide. Where had that come from? Someplace deep inside that craved him at my mercy, where he could deny me nothing. Demand nothing. "You submitted once. I want that again."

He stilled inside me. "That's what you really want?"

I remembered him beneath me, his hands tied to the headboard, muscles straining with unchecked power. Remembered how teasing him to insanity had been the most intoxicating night of my life. His desperation and frustration. The way he'd watched me as I brought myself to orgasm again and again. How he'd given me a piece of himself he'd never planned to give.

Yeah. I wanted that again.

My silence must have been answer enough. He pulled out, lowered me to my feet, and stepped back, appreciation blanketing his face as he studied his helpless slave whose body begged for whatever he was willing to give.

He rubbed his jaw, considering. "If you can go the whole week without coming, I'll think about it."

My jaw about dropped to my breasts.

"But don't think I'll make it easy," he warned. "I'll have you out of your mind with needing to come before the week's over."

My need for him shuddered in my core, and I moaned, a moment away from pleading with him. "A whole week?"

He couldn't be serious. Neither one of us would make it.

But he nodded, fell to his knees, and brought his fingers to my mound, spreading my wet lips. "This will be the ultimate test of control, don't you think, Kayla?" He raised a brow. A challenge. "Can you handle it?"

My nipples peaked, and my chest rose and fell too fast. With a sigh, I let the back of my head thump against the wall. "Can you, Master?"

"I won't deny that it'll be a challenge." He ran a finger up my slit, drawing a tremor from my bones. "But you know I can never resist a challenge." His lips curved into his devil's grin, then he leaned forward and sucked my clit into his wicked mouth.

5. SUMMONS

Monday morning arrived with rain. The deluge gushed from the sky, leaving pools of water that tempted little feet to splash through them. Eve thought about it, but a stern look from me changed her mind.

I blew kisses to her as she climbed the stairs of the school bus, her sneakers lighting up with each step. After the bus disappeared down the road, I returned to the house. No matter how hard I tried, I couldn't displace the feeling of dread settling in my gut.

Gage still hadn't left for work.

Ian still wanted to meet today in his office.

I wanted to crawl back into bed and sleep the dilemma away.

No such luck. I found Gage in his pajamas. He sat on a bar stool in the kitchen, reading the newspaper and sipping coffee.

"Running late this morning?" I asked, rinsing the few dishes left over from breakfast.

"I'm the boss. I'm never late." I heard the bar stool

scrape across the floor, followed by his quiet steps bringing him closer. "It's a hard decision, choosing between work and chaining you up in the basement."

A plate slipped from my sudsy hands and clanked into the sink. Luckily, it didn't break.

He pressed his lips to the side of my neck, his warm breath inducing a delicious shiver. "I want to spend some time with you, just the two of us. In fact, I plan on spending a lot of time with you this week." He leaned into me the slightest bit, his cock nudging my ass. "I've been hard all morning, Kayla. Do you know how difficult it is not to bend you over and fuck you right now?"

I clutched the edge of the sink, biting back a groan. He ran his fingers through my hair, taunting with what I would miss this week.

"I need a cold shower," he muttered, backing away. "When you're done in here, I want you on your knees in our bedroom."

"O-okay." My heart battered my ribcage long after he left the kitchen. I finished loading the dishwasher, then for a few moments, I gripped the counter. Let it prop me up. Once again, I couldn't ignore the hunch that he was punishing me. Was he playing a cruel game? A game designed to mess with my head?

Psychological instead of physical.

Or was he simply amping up his need to conquer and control, and my guilt was wreaking havoc by making me read more into his behavior? Either way, I was frozen. Under his thumb, life had become restrictive and suffocating.

But it's never dull.

Sometimes, that voice in my head was too fucking right. I tuned into the sound of the dishwasher and let the steady *swoosh swoosh* calm my nerves, let it wash away the annoying voices in my head. I was supposed to be somewhere today, but that wasn't going to happen since he'd forbidden me to leave the house this week.

Taking a detour to the foyer, I grabbed my phone from the table and crept down the hall toward our bedroom. As I peered through the door, my cell pressed to one ear while I listened for the sound of the shower, Simone answered with her usual to-the-point greeting.

"Hey," I said, keeping my voice low. "I can't come in this week."

A pause came over the line, and even though Simone wasn't standing in front of me, I imagined her dark blond brows furrowing. "Why?"

Her suspicious tone pricked at my defenses, and I let out a sigh, growing tired of arguing with her about my marriage. But she was the only person who knew of the type of relationship Gage and I had…besides Ian, but I didn't want to think about him or how I'd done the unthinkable by seeing him over the weekend. Or how I was tempted to do something even more stupid, like see him again.

"Something came up. I'm sorry."

"You mean Gage came up. Is his dick more important that those kids?"

"That is—" *Not fair.* Shit. His cock wasn't even an issue right now since he had no intention of fucking me until our anniversary. And those kids...they *were* important. So important that I'd gone to great lengths to hide my volunteer work from my husband because no amount of logic would penetrate his thick skull when it came to my being in the same building as his brother twice a week.

Sick children or not.

"I'll be back next week." I owed Simone more than I could ever repay. She'd been Eve's favorite nurse in the hospital. And she'd become a true friend since I'd married Gage. The kind of friend I talked to, which didn't always work in my favor at times like these. I'd shared too much of my life with her, and she didn't always "get it."

She didn't understand that I owed Gage even more. He would own every part of me until the day I died.

"Damn it, Kayla. I promised Emma you were coming in this morning. Your visits are the highlight of her week."

Simone's words fisted my heart. I remembered Eve in that hospital, alone and scared because I hadn't been there when she needed me. I'd been too busy selling my soul to the devil to save her. Emma spent a lot of time alone in that place too, since her mother was a single parent who couldn't afford to miss work. Nurses and volunteers helped fill that gap, just like they had for Eve.

Emma was only six, the same age as Eve. And she could die...like Eve almost had.

"I'll try to stop in today for a little while. I want to be there."

"Then be here. This is ridiculous. You're a grown

woman. When the hell are you gonna stand up to him?"

"It's not that simple."

"Yes, it is. He either respects you, or you walk. You can't get much simpler than that."

She'd never felt the need to hold back. Simone told it like she saw it, right or wrong.

"Gage is complex."

"I don't care if he's Jesus. How can you justify his behavior?"

I ground my teeth and counted to ten. "I knew what to expect the day I married him. Nothing about him has changed." I was beginning to sound like a fucking broken record.

"But *you've* changed. I see how unhappy you are. You might have agreed to this insane arrangement the day you married the bastard, but you're not happy about it now."

"You don't need to resort to name calling."

"Look," she said in a clipped tone. "You're my friend, so that means I'm going to have your back no matter what. But—"

"There's always a 'but,'" I interrupted.

"*But,*" she began, "you deserve more than this. After everything you went through with Eve, you deserve to be happy. You deserve to be safe."

So did Eve, and that's what Simone and Ian didn't understand. Gage made *her* happy. So how could I justify walking away when things got bumpy, knowing that it would devastate her?

I couldn't.

"I'm sorry." I peeked through the ajar door and saw

steam rolling from the bathroom. So much for the cold shower. "Tell Emma I'll try to visit today. If I can't, I'll make it up to her. I won't let her down."

"You just did."

I couldn't argue with her because she was right. Not only was I disappointing a little girl fighting to live, but I was disappointing myself. Disappointed *in* myself. Disgusted, even. What happened to the ballsy woman who'd stood up to him that first night in the basement? The first night he'd fucked me.

Raped you, the voice of reason whispered in my ear.

That night felt like a lifetime ago.

The spray of the shower shut off, and a few seconds later he entered the bedroom wearing a towel around his waist. I relaxed my face, willing my mask of *everything's a-okay* to fall into place, and pushed the door open.

"I've gotta go," I told Simone.

"He's there, isn't he?"

"I'll call you later," I said, skirting her question.

"See?" Her tone came out testy. "You're lying to him about something you shouldn't have to hide in the first place, but mostly, you're lying to yourself."

I had no argument left, so I ended the call and calmly set the phone on the dresser.

"Was that Simone?" Gage asked, brows furrowing in a way that hinted at his irritation.

"Yeah." I swallowed hard.

"Did you tell her you're not available this week?"

I sat down on the bed and eyed his hard body as he let the towel drop to the floor. "I let her know, but I don't understand why this is an issue." I'd only been a volunteer for a few weeks, but I was growing attached to those kids, and I hated the idea of not being there for them this week, especially Emma.

"Don't argue with me, Kayla," he said, the tick in his jaw speaking volumes. "This week, you're mine and mine alone." He pushed me back onto the mattress and shoved my legs apart. Dropping to his knees, he pulled me toward his face with a rough, demanding grip.

My lips parted, and I closed my eyes as a sigh escaped. His hot breath teased between my thighs, hovering. Barely there, but potent enough to scatter my thoughts.

"I'll forgive you for not greeting me on your knees, seeing as how you were distracted by your *friend*." He shot a hand out and pinched my nipple. Squeezed. Twisted.

I cried out and instinctively tried moving out of reach, but he intensified the pressure between his thumb and forefinger.

"You will not move unless I tell you to. You're going to lie here, spread wide, your cunt aching for my mouth." He nudged my thigh with his nose, drawing a whining plea from my throat. He took my other nipple between two sadistic fingers and pinched.

The pressure was never ending—between my legs and in my nipples. They both ached in two entirely different and unbearable ways. My whole body trembled as I willed it to remain unmoving, even as the vise of his fingers tortured me.

Another small cry tumbled from my disobedient lips.

"Please, Master."

"You desperate little thing," he whispered, his words a heated caress on my pussy. "Fucking turns me on so much." Abruptly, he let me go.

I sat up, placing my weight on my elbows, and watched him through my confusion. He turned his back on me and began dressing. "What are you doing?" I asked.

"Going to work."

Of course he was. I flopped back on the bed and squeezed my eyes shut.

"I'm not touching your sweet cunt, Kayla. And neither are you."

I must have groaned out loud because he laughed. Even when he laughed at me, I found him sexy—that deep and rich sound that shivered along my skin. "You're the devil."

The mattress depressed on either side of my head, and when I opened my eyes, I found his face inches away. Tempting me. Drawing my head up until our lips met.

He moaned into my mouth, and strength seemed to drain from his bones. He blanketed my body, his weight growing heavier by the second. "But I'm your devil. Always, Kayla. I love you so fucking much." Inching back, he gave me a severe look that stole my breath. "You know that, don't you, baby?"

I nodded, barely able to breathe, and somehow managed to tell him that I loved him too. And right then I knew I wouldn't see Ian again. I couldn't do that to Gage, no matter how much his behavior infuriated me.

"Good," he said. "Because I do. There is no one more important to me on this planet than you and Eve."

My body felt like a limp noodle. I remained speechless as he finished dressing. He kissed me one last time before heading toward the bedroom door, adjusting his cufflinks as he strode with purpose.

"I want you to come to the office today. I'll text you." The door shut quietly upon his exit, and I hated myself because I knew what I'd be doing all morning.

Anxiously waiting for the devil to summon me.

6. LUNCHTIME SCANDAL

"Go into the women's restroom on the second floor and touch yourself."

I stopped dead in my tracks in the lobby of Channing Enterprises, and a man in a charcoal power suit almost ran into me from behind. As my cheeks flushed, he strode by me, casting a glare my way. Since standing in the middle of the lobby, unmoving with the phone pressed to my ear, was probably more attention-grabbing than Gage's words, I wandered to the edge and stood in the middle of two towering tree-like plants. Rubbing a leaf between two fingers confirmed they were real.

"Why the second floor?" What a crazy question. My first question should have been *why* at all.

"The PR department takes their lunch about now. I imagine the ladies room will have plenty of activity in it."

"I can't do that in there!" I said in a fierce whisper.

"You can and you will. Tell me when you're in the stall."

Panic ate at my composure. I remained motionless,

eyes unseeing as people bustled around me, their bodies little more than moving blurs.

"Are you moving, Kayla?"

"Yeah." Instead of taking the elevator, I used the stairs, figuring I could at least delay this uncomfortable task for a minute or two longer.

"Taking the stairs won't save you from this." The bastard said it with barely contained amusement.

"I'm in the elevator."

"Do you remember what the punishment is for lying?"

Dread snaked down my spine. "Yes, Master. I'm sorry." I was grateful to be in the stairwell then, where no one else was around to hear me. And I was even more grateful that Gage didn't know the *real* lie. The one I'd perpetrated every day for the past few weeks.

I hefted the door to the second floor open and stepped into the hall. The women's restroom was up ahead to my left, and Gage was right about the busy time of day. Three women entered as I approached. I shouldn't have been surprised though. He knew what went on in this building at all times.

One of the women held the door for me, and as I stepped inside, snippets of conversations filled the space. A toilet flushed and water ran. The hand dryer blew. Maybe I could do what he demanded without being detected since the noise level in here was close to ear-splitting. I entered the last stall and firmly shut the door, double checking the latch.

"I'm here," I whispered.

"Good. Hold the phone with your left hand."

"What if I already am?"

"You aren't."

I swear the man had eyes in the walls of every room. I switched the phone to my left ear. "What now?" I asked in a hushed voice.

"Tease your clit with one finger."

This was beyond humiliating. I shifted inside the stall, standing in the center of the door with my back to it, thankful the stalls were made with privacy in mind; they didn't have gaps between the door and the frame.

My reluctant hand dragged my skirt up my thigh, and I slipped a finger between the lips of my pussy. Heat instantly flared. My head fell back against the door, and I let out a breath.

Two days of being teased and denied. God, this was torture.

"Are you touching yourself?"

"Mmm-hmmm..." Chatter continued on the other side of the door. Gossip about coworkers, stories about the men they were dating, the assholes they'd dumped and the assholes who'd dumped them. I closed my eyes and blocked it all out. Everything but my finger caressing, slipping through the moisture growing between my legs.

"Cup yourself, Kayla." Blocked out everything but Gage's seductive voice in my ear. "Fingers in your cunt, thumb on your clit."

Swallowing a moan, I widened my stance and forced my fingers inside. "Gage..." His name was a breath on my lips. An oath. Bringing my thumb to my clit almost destroyed me, but I did it.

The hand dryer blared on again, and I used it as a cover. "I'm so close."

"I know, baby. That's where I want you. On the edge…" He groaned, and I knew then that he had his cock in his devious hand. His breathing escalated. "Rub yourself and mean it. I want to hear you moan."

I *didn't* want to make a sound. Not with a bunch of gossip mongers who wouldn't hesitate to spread this humiliating task around the office. The flesh under my circling thumb throbbed, skyrocketing my pulse. Biting back a moan, I willed my hips to stay still.

"You're holding back. If you don't moan for me right now, I'll gag you when I get my hands on you."

He knew me too well. The strangled sound escaped my throat just as someone entered the next stall.

"You're very naughty, Kayla." He tsk-tasked. "Touching yourself in the middle of the day and turning me on. Do you know how hard my cock is right now?"

I grunted, unable to do more beyond my constricted throat.

"Do I need to call you into my office for a spanking?"

"Please, Master." The words tore from my tightened lips, breathless enough to count as a whisper. I'd rather he bend me over his desk and whale on me than lose control in this bathroom.

"Fuck, you're sexy. Come to me. Don't wash your hands. I want the smell of your beautiful cunt on your fingers. I want you wet. Do you understand me?"

Several women had exited the bathroom, and the

sudden quiet seemed to echo. I mumbled a yes and ended the call before he could issue another command. Thirty long seconds ticked by as my heartbeat slowed. I straightened my skirt and was about to slide open the lock and push the door open when a single name froze the blood pumping through my veins.

"Did you hear about Katherine Mitchell?"

"Crazy, right?" a woman with a pitchy voice said. "I heard she's coming back."

The sound of rushing water interrupted for a moment. "I'd bet a month's pay the boss is fucking her again."

"Well that's obvious. You don't spend over an hour in his office without him taking out his dick." Laughter echoed. "Rachel told me Mr. Channing's wife disappears in there for *hours* sometimes."

Fire erupted in my stomach, and something dangerous and venomous collided inside me. Possessive jealousy. If I was his and only his, then he was fucking mine and only mine.

"What a pig," one of the women said.

"A hot, rich pig." More giggles. "Think he'll give Katherine the PA position?"

"Ugh. No doubt. That bitch has always had a hold on him."

"It's bullshit. At least four girls have been waiting for a shot at that job."

A door squeaked open then banged shut, muffling the words coming from their running mouths. My cheeks flushing with rage, I tiptoed from the stall I'd been hiding in and faced an empty bathroom.

Listened to the pulse throbbing in my ears.

He was waiting for me, but I didn't want to move. I didn't feel capable of doing anything besides gripping the counter until my knuckles turned white. Their words raped my mind, making me want to claw and scratch and *scream*. They believed he was screwing Katherine. The whole damn building probably thought my husband was fucking another woman.

At some point, I left the bathroom and moved down the hall at a pace that defied the stilettos on my feet. As I waited for the elevator, I practically ripped the shoes off and held them in my shaking fist. No one paid me any attention. I was invisible—just another employee among many. After all, why would the wife of the CEO be on the second floor using the ladies room?

As I rode the elevator to the fourth floor, I couldn't stop the speculation, the mistrust and hurt and jealously from taking hold of me. After our wedding, I'd insisted he transfer Katherine to another office. He'd owed me that much, considering all he'd put me through. Considering all he expected of me. If he wanted control of every aspect of my life, then he could at least give me this.

He'd shocked me by agreeing, by putting *me* first. But he'd brought her back. Why?

Was I not good enough?

The elevator dinged. I despised how my eyes burned with unshed turmoil as I stepped onto the floor where I used to work. The place transported me to the past—to a time I'd been but couldn't quite remember. As if someone else had worked here. Someone who'd been strong and independent.

"Hello, Mrs. Channing. He's waiting for you."

"Thank you," I mumbled to his secretary—a woman who was thankfully married and much older than Gage. I thought I trusted him...I *wanted* to trust him, but my reaction to overhearing the gossip of those women told me otherwise. We were both jealous people. Possessive. Obsessed. Maybe that's why he'd ultimately won my heart, because it recognized its own kind.

Clutching my shoes in one hand, I turned the handle with the other, pushed the door open, and stepped inside.

He sat at his desk—the same one he'd bent me over countless times to ravish or punish. He glanced up as the door clicked shut behind me.

"Took you long enough. Come to me on your hands and knees."

Instead of dropping to the floor, I stood motionless.

He leaned back in his chair and folded his arms. "Kayla, don't make me tell you again."

"Why is Katherine back?"

The question seemed to startle him. "Who told you?"

"It doesn't matter who told me!" My knuckles whitened around the straps of my stilettos. "You promised me she was gone."

He sighed, and the way he did it—as if he were dealing with a recalcitrant child—enraged me. I dropped my shoes so I wouldn't throw them at his smug, I'm-in-charge face.

Bastard.

My vision blurred, narrowed to where he sat as if the walls were closing in on me. Or maybe the memories were coming to claim me. This office held too many of them, most of which were still raw and bleeding. They flooded my mind, flaying me with their brutality. With their sensuality. Me, bent over the desk as his belt punished my ass. On the floor between his knees, eating cock while he ate his turkey on rye.

And the walls...we'd broken in each one. He'd taken me many times in this space, in many ways, from slow and loving to fast and harsh. Time hadn't wiped the slate clean, despite marriage. Despite the fact that I loved this insane man more than he deserved.

Because in that moment, I wanted to kill him.

He studied me for a few seconds—seconds that felt like minutes. Finally, he stood, and rather than beam me with anger and the promise of degradation, his eyes widened in a way that was foreign to me. As if he'd been caught red-handed.

My stomach lurched. Vomit rose. When it came to him, my instincts were usually on the money, and they were screaming bloody murder. I failed to breathe as I brought my hand to my throat, brushing trembling fingers over the collar he'd locked around my neck before we'd married. I had no key to it. He kept it on him at all times.

Because he owned me. Because I was his plaything he kept locked away, ready and available to use and fuck when it suited him. I didn't want to ask, let alone hear the answer, but I had to know.

"Did you sleep with her?"

"God, no, Kayla." He rounded the desk, creeping toward me like one would sneak upon a skittish animal.

I held a hand up. "Don't you dare come near me."

He halted at my venomous tone. "Don't do this, baby. You're overreacting."

His cautious demeanor, and the fact that he didn't have me over his desk, ass reddened from his belt, spoke louder than the thunder in my ears. A tear finally slipped free. Glaring at him, I swiped it away. Pretended it wasn't there.

I wasn't crying. Crying meant he was hurting me, and I'd let him hurt me enough. Day after day, I let him wreck me. Crying meant those women were speaking the truth.

"Why aren't you punishing me, Gage?"

"Seriously? You're picking a fight with me because you want to be punished?" Ignoring my protesting hand, he took a step toward me. Helplessly, I watched him take another, and another until my back hit the door.

Trapped. Nowhere to go. Right back at square one… where I always ended up with him.

He wrenched my arms above my head and shackled my wrists in his strong fist. "Is there a reason you need to be punished?"

"N-no." I hated how shaky my voice was, how the lie seemed to dance off my lips too easily. My face heated, flushing my cheeks with deception.

"You're looking guilty as fuck, Kayla. Are you sure you don't need to be punished?" The uncertainty in his eyes had disappeared. Now that he had me subdued and back under his control, those few moments of unsteady ground he'd stood on were no more. His world was solid again.

Mine was crumbling beneath my feet.

"The thought of you with her kills me." Another tear dripped down my cheek. "Why is she back?"

He brushed the sorrow from my face, and the gesture was so gentle and caring, I wanted to sob. His mouth settled on mine, coaxed my lips apart, plundered away my insecurities. Tightening his hold on my wrists, he shoved his free hand under my shirt and cupped me, thumb whisking the hardened nipple poking through thin silk.

"Gage…" I sighed against his lips, disarmed by his touch. Pliable submissive waiting to bend upon his command. That was me.

"There is no one but you. *No one.*" His gaze sparked with meaning. "Can you say the same?"

"Yes." Though not in the way he meant. Not in the way he was hoping for. No matter how much I loved him, needed him, was bound to him…Ian would always have a tiny piece of my heart. Deep down, he knew that, or he wouldn't have asked.

"You're it for me, baby." His gorgeous blue eyes, fringed by thick lashes that normally shadowed his secrets, held steady. He didn't avoid my gaze, didn't look away in shame or regret. They bespoke truth.

I'd misunderstood. He would build me a new foundation, assure me that I had nothing to fear. Those women were wrong. Katherine wasn't—

"But there is something I need to tell you." He swallowed hard, and my legs almost gave out. If he hadn't pinned me to the door, I would have leaned against it to prop me up.

"Tell me what?" I wanted to take the question back. Wanted to cover my ears and sink through the door to the other side, where I wouldn't hear the words he so clearly didn't want to say. Gage didn't do nervous.

"Katherine's son is mine. That's why she was here the other day. We were arguing over visitation."

A blade sliced through my heart, freshly sharpened. She'd given him the one thing I hadn't been able to. We'd tried. Jesus, we'd tried. Day after day, week after week. We'd fucked more times than most people fucked in a lifetime, yet my curse still showed up like clockwork every month.

"How long have you known?"

"A couple of months." He paused, hesitating. "But I suspected last year after…"

After we lost the baby.

The truth crashed over me. He hadn't believed he could have kids, so finding out the doctors had been wrong—that he was capable of knocking up a woman—had changed everything. Why hadn't I given thought to Katherine's son? I remembered seeing him once, long before Gage had blackmailed me into sexual slavery. Now that I considered it, there had definitely been a resemblance.

How could he have kept something this huge from me? We'd turned a new page the day we married, left the lies and blackmail in the past.

Except you've been lying for weeks.

That annoying voice in my head was right. How hypocritical to feel betrayed when I'd kept something from him as well. Only my lie was small in comparison. I'd only wanted a little freedom. A few stolen hours each week to give something back for the gift I'd been given.

The gift of Eve.

I yanked my hands free and pushed against his chest. "Let me go."

"We need to talk about this."

"No, we don't." Putting all my strength into freeing myself, I shoved him back, inch by hard-won inch, and managed to jerk the door open before he could grab me again. He glanced at the busy room full of his employees, and the boss mask fell into place.

"Don't you dare walk out that door." Though he wore a neutral expression for show, his tone dropped to a range that never failed to ring my warning bells. "We aren't done here, Kayla."

How could he wipe all signs of feeling from his face? Was part of him always pretending? Always keeping an iron grip on control?

"I can't even look at you," I said, not giving a shit if the entire floor heard me.

All sign of pretenses vanished. He tugged me into his office and slammed the door. "How do you address me?"

"You don't get to be my Master today. Today you're just my husband who had a kid with another woman and failed to mention it."

He hauled me to the desk, his fingers grasping my bicep with enough strength to bruise. "You *will* call me Master, even if I have to beat it out of you." He reached for his belt. "Bend the fuck over and lift your skirt."

"No."

His mouth formed a severe line. He wasn't used to being defied. And he hadn't punished me out of anger in so long that the determination in his hands as he unbuckled his belt tore through me. I hadn't stepped out of line since we'd married. Not that he knew of, anyway.

"You don't tell me no." He lunged for me, grabbed a fist full of my hair, and forced me over his desk. My palms slapped the smooth surface. "Fuck, Kayla. Your defiance is only turning me on." He kicked my legs apart and thrust his fingers into me.

I pushed to my toes with a startled cry.

"Who am I?" His grip on my hair tightened.

"A liar."

"Wrong." Slowly, he inched his thumb into my ass, igniting a ring of fire I couldn't escape. My stomach roiled from the intrusion.

"Gage, stop."

"You don't issue the orders. I'm your Master, and if I want to finger your tight little asshole, I will."

I struggled for about two seconds before flopping onto the desk, my body a boneless mess of defeat. Fighting him only prolonged the pain. My breaths blasted the mahogany surface of his workspace. I relaxed my muscles and accepted his probing thumb.

Accepted that I was helpless.

The hardest part of accepting that I was helpless was accepting that I'd put myself in this position. I'd married him when I should have walked. Loved him when I should have hated him. Bent when I should have stood on my own two feet and not only said no, but meant it.

Instead, I found myself bent over with my ass bared. Again. And the truly fucked up part was my body's reaction to everything this man did to me.

"Your cunt is so damn wet, Kayla. It doesn't lie. And that low groaning in the back of your throat? That's you begging me to take you, whether you want to admit it or not."

"Fuck you, Gage."

"You'd like that, wouldn't you? I'm sorry to break it to you, but two of your holes are occupied at the moment, and the only one left is spewing some dirty shit right now."

"Oh my God, you're insufferable."

"Say it, Kayla."

"I'm not calling you Master."

The bastard laughed, and I wondered why until he curled his fingers inside me. His thumb added pressure in my ass that stopped hurting and started feeling *good*.

Damn it.

He was relentless in holding me prisoner on the desk, my hair in his fist and my cheek to the wood. Legs spread wide for his plundering fingers.

I couldn't stop from pushing my ass into him, couldn't hold back a plea for more. Couldn't deny that I wanted him. I *needed* him.

What the fuck was wrong with me?

I had no backbone. That was my problem. Because he had me anytime he wanted, and he knew it. I let out a breath that ruffled my bangs.

"You win, Master. Fuck me. Please, for God's sake, fuck me."

He leaned into my back, his cock pushing against my tender ass where his thumb had been two seconds ago. "Do you remember what I said I'd consider if you made it the whole week without coming?"

My heart skipped a beat. Him, at my mercy. How could I forget? "I remember."

He brought his lips to my ear. "If I fuck you right now, I won't stop until you come. Are you sure you want that?"

Yes, I wanted it. Wanted *him*. But the chance to have the upper hand tempted. Taunted.

"Let me go," I whispered.

He released his grip on my hair and stepped back.

As my blood pumped steady in my veins, I regained my bearings. Regained my damn mind and recalled the reason he'd had me bent over and taking his thumb up my ass.

The words of the grapevine duo tumbled through my head, end over end, an incessant provocation. I rounded on him, anger rushing through me like a flash flood in the bereft of deserts. But the burn in my ass served as an annoying reminder. Screaming at him would accomplish nothing, except for a return to his desk. So I tried leaving, my mouth a straight line to keep my tongue in check.

He blocked my attempts, first stepping to the left then the right.

"Move," I said through gritted teeth. "I'm done here."

His answering smirk grated. "How can you be done? I haven't even started yet."

"You can use sex all you want, but this isn't going away. You have a kid with Katherine. She gave you what I couldn't." What I might never be able to give.

Pain flickered in his eyes, matching the ping in my heart, and I took the opportunity to force my way past, scooping up my shoes on the way to the door. As I reached for the handle, I glanced over my shoulder.

He leaned against the desk's edge, in the place where he'd had me sprawled and vulnerable. "If you walk out, prepare for the consequences when I get home."

I paused, surprised by the way he held on to his executive desk with whitened knuckles. He thrived on control, and right now, he straddled the ledge.

We'd battled, and though he'd won, I wasn't down yet. I threw one last glare in his direction. "Don't hold your breath, Gage. I might not even come home tonight."

7. CRYPTIC

Insufferable didn't come close. Insufferable was the pebble digging into your heel, the itch you couldn't reach to scratch. Insufferable was getting stuck in rush hour traffic with a full bladder and no exit in sight.

Gage's behavior transcended insufferable.

Entering the hospital's lobby, I willed my anger to subside, my pulse to slow. If one good thing had come from our argument, it happened to be that I wasn't sitting at home waiting for him to snap his fingers so I could drop to my knees.

I'd walked out of his office of my own free will, and though part of me dreaded the eventual price I'd pay—taken from my flesh with each agonizing strike of whatever implement he chose—mouthing off to him had been...liberating.

I punched the button for the tenth floor and waited for the arrival of the elevator. Standing up to him had sparked something alive inside me. The woman I used to be, if only for a blip in the grand scheme of things. Being bad hadn't felt this good in such a long time.

I stepped into the elevator and found myself alone until the seventh floor. As the doors slid open, a chill traveled down my spine. I almost expected to find Ian waiting on the other side, just like the other day.

But Ian wasn't there. Two doctors entered, mid-conversation. I tuned out their talk of cancer stages and grades, research, and cutting-edge treatments. Each time I entered this wing, the past threatened to punch through the walls I'd built to protect myself. The memories were never far, and sometimes they crept up on me to bind around my chest until I could hardly breathe.

And that's why coming back to this place was good for me, no matter how difficult. No matter how the antiseptic smell took me back each and every time to the utter despair of Eve's illness. To the hopelessness of watching her become sicker and sicker. To the desperation that had spurred me on to embezzle thousands of dollars from Gage.

If I hadn't stolen the money, he would have never caught me in the act, would have never blackmailed me into loving his sadistic ass. But the most important takeaway from that tumultuous decision was Eve; without my thievery, he would have never moved obstacles to get the care she needed.

The elevator arrived on the children's floor. I stepped out and made my way toward the circular nurse station that served as a hub for activity. A rainbow mural decorated the walls, and the counters of the center island were a mix of complimentary sky blue and shades of gold. The nurses had proudly displayed artwork from some of the children above and below the rainbow. Compared to the rest of the hospital, this floor had the vibe of warmth and innocence.

I spotted Simone immediately. She glanced up from a chart, her reading glasses perched on her dainty nose.

"Emma's been asking for you," she said, tucking a stray blond hair behind her ear.

"Is she awake?"

"Yeah, but she started another round of chemo yesterday, so her spirits are a little low. I'm sure a visit from you will cheer her up."

As I wrung my hands, Simone marked something on a chart, shelved it, then studied me with an assessing eye. "Is everything okay? You seem upset."

"It's nothing. I don't want to get into it right now."

She crossed her arms. "What'd he do this time?"

I blinked, despising the sting in my eyes. My problems were a speck compared the issues these kids faced every day on this floor.

"Hey," Simone said, her voice softening. "I'm sorry. I didn't mean to upset you."

"It's not you." I avoided her gaze and forced myself to pull it together. "Gage and I had an argument. I don't have the energy to talk about it right now, so I'm gonna see if Emma's up for a story."

"That girl is always up for your stories." She squeezed my shoulder. "Let's meet for lunch sometime this week, okay?"

I nodded then headed down the hall, making a stop at

the hand-washing station before stepping into Emma's room. Flowers and stuffed animals covered most of the surfaces, and her mother had brought photos of her siblings from home. I tiptoed to the side of her bed and sank into a chair.

Her lashes fluttered and opened, revealing two brown eyes. A weak smile painted her lips—the only feature brightening her face because she was pale otherwise. But nowhere near lifeless. Not yet. This little girl was a fighter, and she reminded me so much of Eve that coming here was more difficult each time I walked through the door.

Yet I also found it therapeutic in some ways. Bringing a smile to her precious face was my biggest reward.

I picked up the *Cat in the Hat* from her bedside table. "You wanted me to read this one to you next, right?"

She nodded and settled against her pillow. I turned the first page and started reading the story of odd cats and rhymes. After a while, my voice blended with the din of the hospital; the continuous beeping, intercoms, and feet padding down the halls. It was all so achingly familiar.

After a while, Emma's eyelids drooped, but I sensed she was still listening. I read page after page, each word an octave above a whisper. I wasn't sure how long I sat there, content to give her comfort through mere words. Probably no more than twenty minutes, but it felt like an hour. I closed the book and carefully placed it back on the table. Emma's chest rose and fell in steady cycles, her breathing deep and even, indicating she'd succumbed to sleep.

A tingle traveled through my extremities, and that's

when I noticed Ian standing in the doorway. My heart skipped, jumpstarted by the sensation of deja vu.

"You're a natural," he said.

"I wish I could do more for her."

"You're here. That's all you can do, Kayla, and it's enough. More than enough."

I rose and tiptoed across the room, careful not to rouse Emma from her slumber. "What are you doing here?"

"Can we talk for a second?" He nodded toward the hall, and I vacillated between returning to Emma's side, and allowing him to usher me from the room.

The latter prevailed.

I followed him down the hall a few feet, out of earshot of little ears.

"You didn't meet me for lunch," he said.

"I wasn't planning to meet you. I'm just as married today as I was Saturday."

"Normally, that would matter to me."

A doctor approached, and I stepped toward Ian, lowering my voice. "Well, it matters to me."

He brushed his fingers against my cheek. "Do you really want to do this here?"

His touch careened through my system, forbidden and unwanted, but I couldn't displace the familiar longing he'd sparked in me for years. That ember was a shameful entity flaring inside me.

"Why are you doing this?" As I stumbled back, my sneakers squeaked on the linoleum.

He folded my hand in his and refused to let go.

"Come with me?" he asked, though he didn't leave me much choice unless I wanted to risk causing a scene, which I didn't. He pulled me down the hall toward the elevator. I swallowed with a hard gulp, my protests catching in the vise of my constricting throat.

The silence between us grew heavy as we traveled the distance of ten floors. The elevator halted at the bottom, and the doors slid open to reveal the busy lobby. Ian led me past the receptionist and through a double door. We journeyed through a maze of corridors before coming to a halt. He'd switched offices since the last time we'd spoken within the privacy of his workspace.

As he shuffled through his keys, I questioned how I'd ended up *here*. Entering that room was a bad idea, yet my feet had no intention of doing the sensible thing by turning around and navigating the labyrinth of the hospital. My stubborn feet suddenly had a mind of their own, planting me in a precarious situation I didn't want to be in.

He reached for the knob, key shaking in his hand, and missed the keyhole three times before managing to unlock the door. He motioned for me to enter. A small window allowed dreary light in, obscured by the shitty weather. A mixture of paperwork, folders, cups, and office supplies cluttered his desk, which was at odds with his tidy personality.

Ian not only closed the door, but he locked it, and he didn't bother turning on a light. I backed up a step, hating how he stood between me and the exit.

"What do you want?" I asked, folding my arms.

Maybe it was true—curiosity did kill the cat.

I was fucking roadkill then.

"What do you think I want?"

I had no answer. None that I liked, anyway.

"Sit down. I just want to talk." He took me by the elbow and ushered me to the small sofa tucked against one wall. Taken completely off guard, I plopped onto it as he claimed the cushion next to me.

"How is Eve?"

"She's great."

"How are you?" He devoured me with eager, hungry eyes. Despite the low light casting us in shadow, I still clearly saw that he didn't *just* want to talk. He wanted something he couldn't have.

"I'm great. Everything's *great*."

"One big happy family, huh? He hasn't started abusing Eve yet?"

Blistering anger roared through my veins. I moved to stand, but his forearm blocked me.

"It's a valid question, Kayla."

I slapped his arm away. "No, it's not. Do you think I'd allow anyone to hurt my daughter?"

"No, but I never saw you for a doormat either. I never thought you'd go through with the wedding."

I gritted my teeth. "You're about a year too late to question my decisions."

"Better late than never." He leaned in, caging me between his body and the sofa. "You fucked up, Kayla. You let that fucking bastard abuse you. But the real kicker is how you let him near Eve. What the hell is wrong with you?"

I wanted to throw the question back at him, but I couldn't find my voice. His confrontational tone stunned me.

"You sold yourself to save her, but when it comes to him, you put her last." His upper lip curled in a sneer that was foreign to his features. "Fantastic parenting skills there."

My palm sent a sound slap across his cheek. "You don't know shit about my life."

He rubbed his cheek, though he appeared unfazed by my loss of control. "Explain it to me then." He brought his face forward until we were nose to nose.

I placed a hand on his chest, my fingers brushing his stethoscope. I despised the way he had me trapped. Gage had me in this position often—cornered and helpless—but I was used to his overbearing nature, was drawn to his dominance in a way that sickened me if I let myself dwell on it too long.

Ian's behavior unsettled me beyond words, and it wasn't because I didn't like the feel of him being close. With much shame, I realized that I did. No, what sent off my internal alarm was the feeling that something was *wrong*.

I inched back and met his hazel gaze. "Why are you mad at me?"

The festering anger seemed to flee from his bones. He let out a breath. "I'm not mad at you. I'm mad at myself. I should have stopped your wedding, even if it meant crashing it."

"Thank you for not doing that," I said quietly. "I've built a good life with Gage, and Eve is happier than I've ever seen her. She has a father. A *real* father this time. She loves him."

"Do you?" His heartbeat thumped under my palm.

"What type of question is that?"

"One you obviously don't want to answer."

"Because it's none of your damn business." When I got down to the grit of what Gage and I were, love just didn't cover it. What we had was unhealthy and wrong, yet we both thrived on it, craved it, needed it.

"Let me go," I told him. "Being here with you is just…torture. It accomplishes nothing. All we're doing is dredging up the past and hurting each other."

"We don't have to dredge up anything. I'm content to sit here and *not* talk."

I pushed him back an inch. "Ian, stop."

He nuzzled my neck. "Am I making you nervous? Are you feeling things you're not supposed to feel?"

I bit my lip, denying with a quick shake of my head.

"What if you could go back and do it differently?" he asked. "Would you?"

I flipped through the days and weeks and months of the past year, the scenes going off in my mind like flashcards.

My wedding night, when Gage had taken me with the tender patience he rarely allowed me to see.

Our first argument as a married couple. I'd made the mistake of saying hello to the neighbor while checking the mail—the very attractive and very *male* neighbor.

Gage and I had gotten into a shouting match over his ridiculous control issues, and that had resulted in him gagging me until Eve came home hours later. Needless to say, I now steered clear of the neighbor, and I'd been careful to obey since that day.

Until recently, when I'd risked it all to volunteer, knowing full well that Ian worked here. What did that mean? Not for the first time, I wondered what my actions were trying to tell me.

That I missed him?

Definitely.

That I still cared about him?

"I regret many things," I said. "But changing the past isn't possible, and even if it were, I'm not sure I'd want to."

"I think you would." He leaned forward and pressed his lips on mine. The kiss barely lasted a second, but it was enough to knock the air from my lungs.

"Don't," I said through thinly veiled anger.

"You're not the same woman you were a year ago. You're stronger, more determined." He narrowed his eyes. "You're staying for her, aren't you?"

I shook my head, mouth gaping. Was it true? Did I endure Gage's rigid rules and brutal hand for Eve? Or was I staying because no one worked my body the way he did? The heat flaring between my legs—heat that had nothing to do with Ian's brief kiss—gave me my answer. I loved Gage for the way he made me feel; wild and out of control. But I also hated him for the way he made me feel.

Like a caged animal.

Just as Ian was doing now. "I love him."

"I don't believe you."

"You can choose to believe what you want." I shoved him back, surprised by how easily he relented. Compared to Gage, Ian was weak…or less determined to make me bend.

He fell back against the couch, his hand grasping his head. "I'm sorry, Kayla." Wincing, he cursed under his breath. "This is harder than I thought." He was about to say more, but my cell went off.

Gage.

"You going to get that?" Ian asked.

"No," I whispered. "If you need to get something off your chest, do it now." I pointed at the door. "Because once I walk out of here, I'm not coming back." My cell blared again.

Ian rose to his feet. "I can't do this with him calling every fucking thirty seconds."

His constant mood shifts made the hair on the back of my neck stand on end. "Do what?" I stood and faced him, clutching my obnoxious phone like a lifeline. "You're worrying me."

He wasn't acting like himself, and it scared me.

"You know what?" He paused, his attention veering to the ceiling for a moment. "You're right. It's too little, too late. If you're truly happy, then I can accept that. I can leave you be." He exhaled. "I just…I had to know."

I moved to place a hand on his arm but thought better of it. Hell, his cryptic-speak was messing with my head. My phone went off again, and I answered on the second ring with a clipped, "Hello?"

"Where are you?" Gage's question dripped with fury.

"On my way to pick up Eve."

"Don't bother. I picked her up early."

My fingers tightened around the phone. I cast a furtive glance at Ian and noticed the tightness of his features. Afraid he'd see the alarm in my eyes and do something about it—like alert Gage to his presence—I turned my back on him.

"Why did you take her out of school early?"

But I knew the answer before I'd tossed the question out there. He'd done it because maneuvering me was what he did best, and if he wanted me home, getting the upper hand by using Eve would ensure I walked into his trap.

"We need to talk, so get your ass home and maybe I'll go easy on you."

8. SURRENDER

The front door stood between me and my surrender, silently mocking with its facade of normalcy. Beyond that door waited a prison. Waited passion. Waited punishment. Waited *him*.

Most people would stay on the side where I stood. The safe side. The *sane* side. Too bad I needed the insanity to feel sane anymore. Needed his soul-crushing possession to feel free. Because it was freeing...until the last wave of rapture crested and the bars of my world clanked into place again.

Folding my reluctant fingers around the handle, I wedged the door open inch by inch. He had my daughter in there, so entering Gage's domain of fucked-up was a sure thing.

I dawdled in the foyer and hung up my coat, set my purse on the table, fiddled with my wedding ring. The quiet unsettled and that alone sent my feet moving in the direction of the living room, in search of my daughter. Instead, I found Gage on one end of the white sectional, still as stone.

"Where's Eve?"

"In the dining room coloring. She's got a snack, one of those juice pouch thingamabobs you buy her, and enough crayons to draw a rainbow masterpiece." He patted the cushion next to him. "Sit down."

I took a step forward, my gaze on the kitchen. The dining room lay just beyond, irritatingly out of sight.

"For fuck's sake, Kayla." He reached out and planted me on his lap in a way that left no question about his state of mind. I straddled him, and his firm hand on my back brought me closer until my breasts smashed against his chest. His cock throbbed between us, refusing to be ignored.

"Where did you go?"

"The mall." The lie left my lips in a near mechanical way. "Then I went for a drive. I needed some time to think."

With a sigh, he dropped his head against the back of the couch. "I was going to tell you."

"Why didn't you?"

He slid his palms up my thighs and squeezed. "I knew it would hurt like hell. We've been trying for months—"

"Gage...please." Closing my eyes, I pinched the bridge of my nose, sensing the onset of a headache. I didn't want to go down this road. Not today—not when my emotions were a mutilated, bloody mess. Dealing with Ian's cryptic presence and then facing the fact I might never have another child was too much to handle in one day.

"This is why I didn't tell you," he said. "I didn't want to rip that wound open."

"The truth had to come out eventually."

Just as all secrets do.

"I know, Kayla. Fuck. Don't you think I know that? I wanted to give us time…I was hoping…never mind."

What he didn't say busted through with clarity. He'd banked on the appearance of two lines to soften the blow when he told me about his child with *Katherine.*

Katherine, of all people.

My stomach lurched. God, how I hated that woman. I could already imagine the smug curve of her lips. She'd hold this over my head, milk it for all it was worth. She was the mother of his child…and I wasn't.

But I *was* his wife. He'd put his ring on my finger. He shared a bed with me every night. He got what he needed every time he took his belt to my ass. Every time he pushed me to my knees, past my limits. Every time he fucked me. Suddenly, I wanted to curl up at his feet and beg him to do as he wished.

I had power.

My mind turned itself inside out mulling over the realization. She had his son, but I had him where it counted—I had him by his obsession, by his heart, *and* by his balls.

And now I had his mouth opening under mine, allowing me two seconds to claim until he rose up from rock-bottom and remembered who he was. He held me by the nape and took control, plundering my mouth in a way that only Gage could. The taste of him on my tongue pounded the memory of Ian's chaste kiss to dust.

I completely lost my shit, grinding my slick pussy against the bulge in his pants. He swallowed my moans, let loose one of his own, then abruptly broke free. He glanced down at our bodies, practically interlocked despite our clothing.

"Don't think this changes anything." He brought his lips to my ear. "Your hot little cunt won't tempt me," he whispered. "No orgasms."

My head was still spinning from dry-humping him like a horny teen, but at least I was lucid enough to catch what he'd said. To grasp the meaning of it.

"No?" I challenged, moving my hips.

He shook his head. "It's going to be torture, Kayla."

My eyes drifted shut. "Why's that?"

"You're in big trouble," he said, palming my breasts, "and your punishment is going to make my cock throb like hell."

I groaned, knowing that I couldn't throw his deceit in his face without my conscience lambasting me.

"But we're getting sidetracked here, aren't we?" He let his hands drop. "You might not believe it, but I *am* sorry. You deserved the truth."

I'd never felt shittier than I did in that moment. This was a rare occasion for Gage. What had gone down in his office earlier today had knocked him off his game, and he was still reeling.

"So she's not coming back to work for you?"

"No, baby."

A lengthy pause fell upon us, and I sensed the wheels

in his head turning.

"We'll tell Eve together. But I think it would be better for her to get to know him first. He's about her age, and for all intent and purposes, he's her brother."

"That bitch's spawn is *not* Eve's brother."

Gage narrowed his eyes. "He's part of me too. I realize we have a lot to deal with, but don't take your hatred for Katherine out on my son."

I pushed off his lap and wandered around the living room, since in a way, it beat pacing. This would change everything. Later it would really hit me. I felt the weight of his keen gaze on me, so I gave him my back and folded myself in the protection of my arms.

But then he had to go and melt my heart by embracing me from behind. By showing me we were in this together. "Baby, you're strong and compassionate and caring. I know you'll accept him as your own."

The way he'd accepted Eve as his own. He didn't have to voice it. I heard the truth.

"Are you going for custody?"

"I won't take him from his mother, but I do want to be part of his life." His arms tightened around me. "I want the three of us to be part of his life."

"Like one happy family, in between the whips and chains."

His low laugh vibrated against my neck. "Whips, chains, and nipple clamps. Don't think I've forgotten how you stormed from my office earlier."

The doorbell rang, fracturing our private bubble.

Eve raced from the kitchen. "Is that Leah?" she asked

as Gage let me go. I cast a confused glance in his direction, one bordering on suspicious.

He eyed me in a way that set my teeth on edge. "No, princess. There's someone I want you to meet."

The world seemed to freeze as he disappeared into the foyer. When he returned, ushering Katherine and her son into our house, the earth lurched forward again with too much force.

Oh hell no.

I would not let that woman get under my skin in my own home. Rather than avoid her gaze, I met it head-on, refusing to let her haughty expression draw a response from me. I'd expected her nasty disposition, had prepared for it from the moment I learned Gage was her son's father. All I had to do was remind myself that his pants were still damp from my arousal. I hoped the bitch smelled it, tasted it on her vapid tongue.

Folding my arms, I clenched my teeth as I watched them interact. Eve warmed to her son immediately, which wasn't surprising because she welcomed everyone. Katherine took a step closer to Gage and opened her mouth, about to spew her venom, but he halted her with a raised hand.

"This isn't the time or place."

Just like that, she clamped her lips shut and fumed in silence.

He returned his attention to the kids and spoke to Eve. "You're going to spend the day with Katherine and Conner."

His words were a jolt to my system. I lurched

forward, hands fisted at my sides, about to shout my disapproval, but Eve's expectant face cooled my wrath. "She's not going anywhere with that woman."

Gage threw me a dark glance. A warning to behave. "We aren't discussing this right now."

"But—"

"Not now," he said in a tone that proved more effective than him raising a hand.

Now I was the one fuming in silence.

"Mommy, can I go?"

Biting my tongue, I nodded.

"But what about game night? Today is Monday," she said with pride.

Gage bent so he could meet her eyes. "You're going to have game night with them."

"Are you and Mommy coming?"

"Not this time, princess. Your mom and I have a date." He tilted his head. "Do you know what a date is?"

She shook her head, curiosity and dejection coloring her features.

"A date is when two people go out and do something special."

"Like what?"

Gage glanced at me, his grin hinting at a devious plan brewing in his mind. "I can't say. We wouldn't want to ruin the surprise for your mom, would we?"

Katherine glowered at me. If looks could maim, I'd be a pile of shredded skin and bones. Gage's words cooled my ire some because he'd not only put her in her place with a lift of his authoritative hand, but he'd shown her beyond doubt that she had no place between us.

She left with her son, taking Eve with them, and my spirits plummeted. Gnashing teeth seemed to take over my gut, cutting me to pieces. Knowing that she was walking out the door with my baby girl and watching her do it were two different things.

The resulting disquiet scraped my mind like claws on a chalkboard. I crossed my arms. "You should have asked me before you let that bitch take my daughter." I didn't want Eve around her. Hell, I didn't want *him* around the bitch.

"I thought she was *our* daughter."

"She is." I dipped my head. "You know you're the only father she has."

"And I'll make decisions for her, same as you." He lifted my chin. "If I thought Katherine posed a risk to Eve, I'd be the first in line to do something about it." The firm set of his mouth softened. "This is more about jealousy than anything. I know you well."

I couldn't deny it, as she'd been nothing but kind to Eve in the past.

"Don't think I've forgotten about your tantrum in my office." His fingers tightened around my chin. "On your knees, now."

Strength trickled from my body, escaping through the holes he'd poked in my armor. I dropped and assumed the position. He stood before me, his feet planted with grating confidence shoulder-width apart on the floor.

"Kayla."

I peered up through the strands falling over my right

eye. The ones he brushed away with a touch so soft and gentle, it stole my breath. "Yes, Master?"

The corner of his mouth quirked up, and I knew I'd hit the right button. He was helpless against that title when I gave it to him of my own free will. It was one of the few ways I had of manipulating him.

Tucking my hair behind my ear, he moved even closer. Caging me in. Making my world narrow to the hard floor under my knees, the blazing warmth in my extremities, and the larger-than-life posture of the man who owned me.

"I'm in a merciful mood, so you're spared from taking a lashing." He reached into his pocket and dangled a set of nipple clamps at eye level. Upon further inspection, I realized they were the kind he reserved for going out. The kind that made me feel beautiful, despite the agonizing pain they caused.

"However, I think you deserve these. What do you think, Kayla?"

If I disagreed with him, he'd only lash me for it, and my nipples would still end up between his sadistic vises. "Yes, Master. I deserve them."

"Go into our bedroom and prepare for me. I left the coconut bath products out for you." He fisted the clamping set. "I expect you on your knees, naked, no later than thirty minutes from now. Do not move from that position." He pivoted and headed into the kitchen.

As I dragged my feet toward the hall, I spied him opening a bottle of his favorite red. He perched on a bar stool and made himself comfortable as if he intended to stay put for a while. He'd probably sit there for at least an hour, his cock growing thicker, straining against his pants, forming a hard ridge behind his zipper at the thought of me on my knees in the next room.

On my knees waiting for him. Hurting for him. Powerless to do anything other than pass the time in supplication.

I entered the bedroom and quietly shut the door. Thirty minutes didn't give me much time to bathe, shave my legs, do something with my hair.

But he'd expect me to look like a damn model anyway. I shook my head, kicking myself for feeling a modicum of surprise. Gage had never made my life easy, and he never would. His talents lay in other areas, like making me insane with want and need when he got me under his powerful body in bed, up against the wall, bent over a table...chained to the St. Andrew's cross.

Humiliated on my knees with his cock on my tongue.

I sighed as I switched on the faucet to the tub. Despite all that, he made me feel loved. Cherished. Possessed. There wasn't anything he wouldn't do to have me, to fight for me, to protect me. He would crash into hell and charm the devil out of his throne if it meant giving me the world. Of course, he'd chain me to it. The world and I...we were both treasured possessions in Gage's fist.

I shut the faucet off, twisted my hair into a messy up-do, and sank into the blessed hot water. I wanted to lean my head back and close my eyes for a few minutes—just long enough to prepare myself for whatever he had planned. But I couldn't. Every minute counted. Two minutes to shave the barely-there stubble on my legs. Another minute lathering my steaming skin with the coconut body wash he'd left on the edge of the tub.

Ten more minutes to dry off and spread lotion on every inch of my skin. What little time I had left, I used for hair and makeup, and at the thirty-minute mark, I dropped to my knees in the middle of the bedroom and watched the clock to pass the time. No matter how much I pleaded with him to lay a rug down, he refused. The sadist in him gleefully smiled at my pain.

He appeared in the doorway forty-five minutes later, and my knees ached something fierce as he laid the clamps, along with a butt plug, onto the bed. He disappeared into the walk-in closet and emerged a few minutes later wearing tan slacks paired with a soft navy knit shirt. He'd left three buttons at the neckline open. Damn, I wanted to kiss down his throat and make him moan. Gage's idea of casual was no less arresting than the business suits he wore to the office.

"What have you learned from this?" he asked as he wandered to where I knelt.

"To obey you." The strong, more recent voice in my head rebelled, threatening to throw a verbal punch at his beautiful face.

He reached out and pulled me to my feet, and his eyes sizzled as he scoured my body with a single glance. "God, I'll never get over how gorgeous you are."

His words cast a sheen of desire down my spine. "Same here," I whispered.

Reaching for the clamps, he smiled. "Is your cunt wet, Kayla?"

"Yes."

"Yes what?"

"Yes, Master."

He gestured to my chest. "Present your breasts."

Pulling my shoulders back, I thrust them forward, peaks hard and tingling at just the thought of him clamping them. The fierce pinch would hurt like hell and cool the fire between my legs.

He held up the jeweled chain, and I lifted my chin to allow him access to the discreet built-in ring in my infinity collar. He attached the top of the contraption to the collar, and dainty layers of chains draped my chest. At first glance, people would think it was an elaborate necklace. But if they looked closer, they'd noticed two single chains lowering between the valley of cleavage.

He took a nipple between two fingers and rolled with a light caress. He did the same to the other side, making them extra sensitive, causing an ache that would intensify the sting once he tightened the clamps. Gage often found reasons to punish me so he could play with my nipples in his most favorite and sadistic way.

"These belong to me. Your cunt belongs to me. Don't ever forget that." He pressed one vise against a tingling bud and closed the prongs. A sharp twinge shot through me, coalescing at the tip of my breast.

"I'm the Master of your pain, the Master of your pleasure." He clamped the other side, eliciting a whimper.

"Loosen them, Master. Please," I whispered, barely

able to catch my breath. Stones the color of his sapphire eyes dangled, and the added weight heightened my agony.

"Sorry, baby. You're going to suffer tonight." He held my chin in his hand—his modus operandi when it came to putting me in my place. "Don't you ever walk out on me like that again."

What he wanted was an apology, but he wouldn't get one. My nipples throbbed, leaving me with nothing nice to say, so I said nothing at all.

Pulling another clamp from his pocket, he bent and gathered the two sapphire stones together. He attached the additional chain to the tiny hooks at the ends, and the chain tickled my belly.

I watched him in fear and a little wonder as he spread the lips of my sex and placed the third clamp. I gave out a stunned cry, but instead of the familiar sharp ache I expected, that contraption between my legs felt so damn good. Too good. One glance into his eyes told me that was his intention.

To keep me on edge, aroused with no end in sight, my nipples connected to my clit. Pain connected to pleasure. All of his toys chained together for his gratification.

The next five days until our anniversary seemed to span for decades.

Sliding his palms up my thighs, Gage remained kneeling on the floor. I lost my breath because it wasn't often that I had my husband on his knees at my feet. An expression of awe blanketed his face. His eyes heated, darkened to indigo, and the need for control arose in me once again.

I wanted to dominate him.

Wanted to make him writhe.

Make him howl and beg.

Make him submit to *me*.

Warmth crept up my neck and flushed my cheeks as he stood and reached for the butt plug.

"Bend over," he said, his voice thick with seduction.

I planted my hands on the mattress and gave him my ass. Holy hell, this man was my Master all right. And he was absolutely shameless. I told him as much, to which he laughed as he worked the plug in, using enough lubricant that it wasn't too uncomfortable. But then the thing went off, sending vibrations through every nerve in my lower extremities, and I arched my back, expelling a deep moan.

He whirled me around and pushed me onto the bed, then he pulled a pair of lacy thigh-highs from his pocket. Taking my foot in his hand, he began rolling one up my calf, past my shaking knee until the lace top banded around my thigh. He grazed my pussy with his knuckles for a few laborious seconds before giving my other leg the same treatment.

"You're fucking exquisite." He rose to his full height, rubbing the front of his pants. "A test of control indeed. Finish dressing. Something light with a short skirt that flares. I want easy access to that sweet ass."

Oh my God. My nipples were pinched to the point of numbness, and I couldn't move without my clit aching, but he somehow ignited me with mere words.

Dressing was a no-brainer. A flirty black dress with a draped top to hide the clamps, and a strappy pair of the standard four-inch heels he required I wear most of the time. The simmering lust in his eyes told me I'd chosen the right outfit.

"Ready?" he asked.

Was I? I honestly didn't know, but I took his hand, anxious to find out.

9. THE EDGE OF DECENCY

The restaurant gave off a vibe of sin. Low lighting invited couples to sit close and whisper dirty things to each other. Red walls and sleek black tables made me think of passion and sex. Bypassing the section of tables in the middle of the room, the petite hostess halted at a private dining booth and pulled back a gauzy gold drape.

Dining booth didn't come close. The alcove had all the makings of a place to share a meal, but the horseshoe shape of the black cushions, along with red and gold accent pillows, spoke of something else. Something sinful, dark, and forbidden.

Gage had more than dinner on his mind.

"Mr. Channing, your private dining booth is ready."

Gage gestured for me to slide in before him, all the way to the back wall. As he settled next to me, he ordered a bottle of wine.

"Excellent choice, sir."

The way she said "sir" made me bristle, and I couldn't explain why. I didn't like the flirty smile she aimed at

Gage or the way her cleavage threatened to spill over the white top of her uniform.

"Have you been here before," I asked after the hostess left to fetch our wine.

"A few times, yes."

"With Katherine?"

He frowned. "Do you intend to waste the whole night talking about her?"

I dipped my head, letting my hair hide the flush in my cheeks. "No."

He swept my hair back. "The past doesn't matter, Kayla. There's only now." He turned my face toward him, refusing to let me hide. "No one has ever captivated me the way you do." He leaned forward and brushed his mouth over mine, barely touching, merely hovering with the promise of more.

"The thought of your pretty nipples pinched between my clamps is enough to make me hard. Only you can do that."

Keeping my lips parted, I closed my eyes and breathed him in. Allowed myself to fall into his snare. He lowered a spaghetti strap, his warm fingers trailing over my goose-bumped skin. His touch skimmed over a clamped nipple through my dress.

I sensed the slow unraveling of his control, felt his lips teasing mine, his tongue aching to mate. To own.

The hostess fractured the moment with her presence. "Your wine, sir."

Gage and I broke apart, and I was glad I wasn't the one on the other end of his dark glare. "We require privacy. Announce your presence before entering next time."

"Of course. I'm sorry." But she didn't seem sorry at all as she set two menus onto the glossy table, followed by wine glasses and a bottle of red. I didn't bother reaching for the menu since Gage always ordered for me anyway.

She filled our glasses half full. "Your server will be here momentarily to take your orders." Her red lips curved into a suggestive smile. "Is there anything else I can do for you, sir?"

I swallowed a growl as Gage dismissed her. Silence fell upon us, giving me time to stew over how gorgeous my husband was. He turned heads, commanded respect without earning it. His entire being harvested power and sexual prowess.

Had his jealous streak rubbed off on me?

Our server arrived, and this woman was no less attractive than the hostess, but she showed respect by not openly flirting with a married man. Gage rattled off our orders before she exited through the curtains, leaving us alone again, stowed away in our intimate booth.

"Your jealousy is a major turn-on." He downed his glass of wine in two drinks, which was so unlike him. Then he set the glass down with a heavy hand, leaned back, and lowered his zipper with a taunting smile.

"Come over here and grind on me."

"What?"

He raised a brow. "Did I stutter?"

"N-no." But I couldn't help but observe the people on the other side of the gossamer drapes, their movements resembling shadowed ghosts in the dim restaurant. This place had been designed for public displays of indecency.

Gage took my chin in his firm hand. "The only thing that matters right now is your Master's cock."

I opened and shut my mouth at least three times. I'd married this sex-crazed, brazen man a year ago, yet he still managed to knock me off my axis way too often.

"Kayla, my cock isn't going to fuck itself."

He had no shame. None. Zilch.

"Here?" My eyes shifted around the private space, and I almost expected the waitress to appear.

He thrust his hips the slightest bit, flaunting his hard-on with too much pride. "Yes, *here*." He aimed his patented devil's grin my way. "Now hop on before I bend your sexy ass over the table and take my belt to it." He tilted his head. "Somehow, I think that might gain more attention than you quietly riding my cock."

Swallowing nervously, I stood and was about to lift a leg over his lap to straddle him when he whirled me around and fit my body between his knees. He lifted the back of my dress then pulled me down in one swift motion until his erection nestled against my bare ass. He spread my thighs wide, making me shoot a hand out to grip the table for balance.

"I want deep inside you." His low tone whispered down the side of my neck. "Lift up," he said, hands on my hips. I raised my bottom, and he pulled me down until I sheathed him. And we both moaned, on the brink of madness.

I arched my spine and sank against him, back to chest. He ran his fingers down my thighs, teasing with each inch of material he touched before he reached underneath my skirt and carefully removed the clit clamp.

"Ow!"

"Shh," he said. "Unless you want to be heard." His tone was much too satisfied.

I breathed noisily, trying to survive the sudden rush of blood to my pussy, and trying not to cry out again.

"This isn't so bad, is it? I might just eat my dinner like this, with my cock buried inside you." The plug in my ass started vibrating.

"Oh God…"

He wrapped his arms around my waist, remote to the plug clutched in his hand, and rested his chin on my shoulder. "Can you stand it, Kayla? Me inside you like this? Can you stand the thought that when the server brings our dinner, she'll see you spread and sitting on my cock with nothing but your skirt hiding your beautiful cunt?" He stroked my throbbing clit. "Hiding the way our bodies are joined."

"You wouldn't!"

"You said I'm shameless. I'm about to prove you right."

"Why are you doing this?"

"I take great pleasure in making you squirm." He tilted my head back, and his mouth opened over my throat, left a wet trail to my ear.

"Mmmmm…" I lifted my hips the slightest bit, aching to feel him pushing in and out, rubbing that mystical spot that sent me out of my mind every time.

"Damn, Kayla." His breath blasted my neck, and his hands returned to my hips. "Fuck me to the edge."

I lifted then sank back onto his cock, the table shaking under my grip. "What if I can't stop? It's been days. I don't know—"

He bounced my body up and down, cutting off whatever I'd been about to say.

"More," he groaned, yanking me down to glove him again. "Give it all to me. Everything but your orgasm, baby. Save that for our anniversary."

I melted into him, not only molten lava between my legs but deeply touched by his words. This meant something to him. Beyond the sexual games, the teasing and denial, lived a man who wanted to make a single night special. Memorable.

I gently rode him, my hips swiveling at a steady pace that brought him deep inside me on each rotation. The point of no return neared for us both. But I wouldn't stop until he told me to. My job was to take his cock for as long as he wished, as deep as he wanted, and hold back my orgasm.

And holding back would give me the ultimate prize— his submission for a night. He hadn't been kidding though when he said he wouldn't make it easy. He slipped his fingers under my dress, up my sides, and unclamped my nipples. Blood rushed my sensitized peaks, and a hoarse cry escaped my throat.

"Keep fucking me, baby."

I hadn't realized I'd stopped. I pushed upward then

impaled myself on him again, making him moan. God, how I wanted to send him hurtling over the edge, take control from his iron-willed fist.

"Harder," he growled, taking my nipples between his fingers.

A desperate plea fell from my lips. Desperate and treacherous. I couldn't let him win this cruel game. The stakes were too high, meant too much.

"I mean it. Fuck me until you're there. I can wait on the edge for hours. Can you?"

Frustrated tears slipped from my eyes. Gage had practiced the art of control for years, and I was weak in comparison. He'd won this battle before it had begun.

"Take my cock like you mean it." He tweaked my nipples with teasing fingers, keeping time to my undulating hips.

"Please, don't make me come."

"That's a first. You usually beg for the opposite." He grabbed my earlobe with his teeth, pulled, then let go. "But you want something, don't you?"

"Yes!"

"Yes, what?"

"Yes, Master."

"Tell me what you want again. This time in detail."

Drawing an unsteady breath, I visualized it, held onto it, and willed my body to stay strong.

Don't give in.

"I want you tied to the bed, naked. Unable to move."

"What else?"

"I want to suck your cock for hours, but I won't let

you come."

I'd make him *hurt*. He'd regret every wretched thing he'd ever done to me.

"I believe you have a little sadist in you, Kayla. What else?"

"I want you gagged, blindfolded."

Helpless.

He grabbed my hips and yanked my body down with a vicious thrust. "I should make you come right now just to end this madness."

The idea of a role reversal unhinged him, made him grasp for the upper hand. A year ago, he'd promised his submission was a one-time deal, and he intended to hold to that promise, even if it meant fighting dirty. A blizzard would grace hell before he'd willingly give me control again.

He not only meant to push me to the edge, but he meant to throw me off without a parachute. Thank God our dinner beckoned because I was ready to leap, to hell with the consequences.

10. CROSSROADS

Beyond frustrated from Gage's week of sexual games, I gave caution the finger and took a logic-defying risk on Friday morning.

I went in for my shift at the hospital.

If Gage found out, it would ruin our first anniversary. But I was going stir crazy in that house, cooped up like Rapunzel. Only I wasn't a girl held captive by an evil sorceress that thirsted for power. I was a sex slave held prisoner by my husband's deviant desires.

He'd given me explicit instructions with no room for bending the rules, yet here I was, not only at the hospital to see Emma, but I was sticking around afterward to have lunch with Simone. I entered the cafeteria, attention on my cell as I read the text Simone had sent, telling me she'd snagged us a table. Two steps into the busy hub of the hospital at lunchtime, and I collided with a warm body.

I lifted my head and took in Ian's masculine jawline, shadowed with stubble. Forgoing his normal white doctor's coat, today he wore teal scrubs.

"Excuse me," I muttered, veering to the right and attempting to go around him.

He followed my movement. "Do you have a minute?"

I'd managed to avoid him for weeks, but now everywhere I turned, he was in my way. Literally. "There's nothing left to say."

"I know where I stand, Kayla. Is it too much to ask that you have lunch with me?" His mouth quirked in an endearing way. A sexy way.

I couldn't do this. He was trying so hard to squirm back into my life, but he was wasting his time. Folding my arms, I focused on his chest. "We can't be friends."

"Because of Gage?"

"Yes, because of Gage. He's not okay with this."

"I don't give a fuck what he's okay with." He tilted my chin. "You shouldn't care either. Are you not your own person anymore?"

I frowned, once again thrown off by his odd mood swings. "I'm not doing this with you."

"Doing what? Getting a harsh dose of truth? Or sharing a meal?"

"Take your pick. Besides, I'm meeting someone, so if you'll excuse me...?" I stared him down.

"Your wish is my command." His barbed tone pricked at my roller-coaster emotions. God, the way he spoke to me hurt. He stepped to the side and swung an arm out in a display of grand gesture, his body language screaming at me.

Go on, he silently taunted. *Pretend I don't exist.*

His presence shook me up, made me want to bolt, but I wouldn't give him the satisfaction of knowing his words chewed my heart up and spit it out. I went through the lunch line in a blur, my spine tingling with the notion that he was watching me. I turned around and scanned the raucous room, but he'd disappeared. Instead, I spotted Simone, who raised a questioning brow.

Carrying my food, I squeezed between tables, went around a small group of nurses chatting, and settled into the seat across from her.

"How do you know Dr. Kaplan?" she asked as she dipped a chicken strip into a ranch cup. She could put the king of junk food junkies to shame, yet she never gained a pound.

"I met him in college." Stirring my soup with a spoon, I wished like hell she wouldn't press for more info.

She narrowed her brown eyes. "Now that I think of it, I do recall him hanging around Eve's room. He sat with her a lot while you were gone."

That reminder only made me feel like shit. Ian was kind and caring and fucking sane. Gage was the opposite of all those things.

"So what's the story there?" she asked.

"There's not much to tell."

"Uh-uh. You're not playing the vague card on this one."

Spooning up a bite of chicken noodle soup, I blew on it. "He's Gage's brother."

"Get the hell out. No way."

"Yes way." I sipped on my hot soup for a couple of

minutes, Simone giving me the stare-down the whole time.

"C'mon, gimme the 4-11. Did you and Dr. Kaplan have a *thing*?"

"Why would you think that?"

She raised a brow. "You wear everything on your face, Kayla."

Funny. Gage told me the same thing once.

"I guess you could call it a thing." I nibbled my lip, debating on how much to tell her. "I was in love with him."

"This is getting juicier by the second. Dr. Kaplan is a sweetheart. So what happened?"

"My ex-husband happened."

Simone was aware of my history with Eve's biological father…Eve's sperm donor. DNA didn't make a father. Being there did. Loving and caring and giving *time* to a child made a father.

Gage was that to Eve.

"When did you meet Brother Number Two?"

"A few years ago. He hired me on as his personal assistant." I pushed a bite of salad into my mouth and chewed. Simone didn't know about the blackmail or the kidnapping, and she didn't know that Gage had paid for Eve's care. Very few people did, as he'd gone to great lengths to remain an anonymous benefactor.

"So you ended up falling for both of them." She mulled over that piece of information for a bit. "Looks like Dr. Kaplan still has a thing for you." She pointed to my left hand. "Regardless of that shackle on your finger.

That's why you're hiding your shifts here from Gage, isn't it? There's still something between you and that fine specimen of a doctor."

"Not on my end," I said, my cheeks flushing, contradicting the denial. "Things are complicated." What a clichéd cop-out.

Simone shook her head. "Your life is like a soap opera, only more entertaining." She glanced toward the entrance of the cafeteria, where I'd run into Ian. "Do you ever wonder if you made a mistake?" She shrugged her shoulders. "Maybe you're with the wrong brother."

"Jesus, Simone. Gage is my *husband*. Not some guy I've been dating for a few weeks."

"He's cold and distant. Does his heart even beat?"

Letting out a frustrated breath, I swept my bangs to the side. "You met him once. I don't think you can judge the character of someone during a single dinner."

"It's called intuition. I don't know what happened to yours, but when it comes to him, you can't see shit."

I wouldn't bother telling her that Gage didn't care for her either. She was too crass for his taste, too immodest. Mostly, she was too independent—a trait Gage did *not* find attractive in a woman.

He wouldn't like the rebellious streak of independence sparking to life inside of me either. These last few weeks reminded me of how amazing it felt to go places, talk to people, order my own food, and wear whatever the hell I wanted before I'd said "I do" and gave those things to my husband. I just didn't know how to voice what was in my heart because anytime I came close, he turned me to mush with the way he adored me, lusted after me, and made me feel like I was the only woman in his world.

Except I wasn't the only woman in his world. Katherine was the mother of his child. What little soup and salad I'd eaten threatened to come back up.

Simone frowned as if she saw the turmoil darkening my face. I didn't like the pity straining her features.

"You've got serious baggage, girl." She picked up a French fry and chewed, her forehead creased in contemplation. "If you want your marriage to work, you need to tell him. Sneaking around like this isn't good for the soul." Simone had stood by her opinion since the day I'd decided to volunteer at the hospital.

Since the day I confided the nature of my relationship with Gage, because I'd needed to use her as a cover. She genuinely cared about people, which made her a damn good nurse. She'd cared enough about me to lie on my behalf, to play the part of yoga companion.

"I know I need to tell him."

"So bite the bullet and tell him, and don't back down."

"He won't give permission for this. Not as long as Ian works here."

"Uh-uh." A low growl escaped her mouth. "I'm not talking about getting his fucking permission. Don't let him railroad you. If he really loves you, as you say he does, then he'll want to see you happy."

The subject of Gage never failed to rile her up. She was headstrong, self-sufficient, and no man would ever make her kneel at his feet.

Of this, I was sure.

I picked at my salad, and for a few minutes, the din of the cafeteria lulled me into a state of calm. I loved being in the thick of people. Loved the dichotomy of voices that filled the space, making my chaotic thought processes fall silent.

"What if he can't accept it?"

"Then you and Eve are always welcome at my house."

A tumultuous story tainted her past. I was sure of it. A story that had left her battered. But she didn't talk about her life much, or the scars I sensed she carried around with her. Maybe I recognized myself in her, except she was strong where I was weak. She stood on her own two feet while I dropped to my knees on a daily basis.

I envied her, yet I wouldn't change who Gage was for anything. I wanted him to give me some slack—not become someone else. Embracing my submissive nature was liberating.

I just needed…more.

I needed to tell him everything, then maybe I could breathe again. The idea of this hanging over my head the whole weekend while we celebrated our first anniversary suffocated me.

"You're right. Lying to him is eating me alive." I took a long swig of my water to quench my suddenly parched throat. "I think I'll drop by his office. It's going to be hard as hell, but getting this off my chest before we go away for the weekend is the right thing to do." I scooted back and rose to my feet.

Maybe he wouldn't come undone with his employees on the other side of the door. Right. And maybe I'd hallucinated him bending me over his desk and forcing his thumb up my ass. It wouldn't matter where we were when I spilled my guts.

"Don't back down. Make him respect you." She pounded a fist against her palm. "If you need me to beat him up, I'm more than willing."

The idea of a woman beating Gage was laughable. "Thanks for the pep talk."

"Anytime. Let me know how it goes."

I emptied my trash and placed my dishes in the respective bins before leaving the way I'd come. As I made my way through the hospital toward the main entrance, I expected to find Ian waiting around every corner.

As if he were stalking me and waiting to pounce.

I was losing my damn mind. When I'd first started at the hospital, I'd known running into him was a possibility. So why had I done it? Gage would want an answer to that same question, but I didn't have one.

11. TIRADE

Maybe the real question I should have asked was why the hell Katherine had her slutty ass planted on my husband's desk. She sat to the side, her perfectly tanned legs crossed toward him, hiking her red skirt up her thigh.

Gage was busy scanning the paperwork in his hands, and Katherine had her back to me, so neither of them noticed my presence.

I stepped inside his office and let the slam of the door announce my arrival. Gage lifted his gaze. Katherine startled, her ass sliding off his desk. She whirled, but when she saw me, her surprised expression turned into one of calculation. A slow smile widened her red lips. She held my gaze as she buttoned the top four buttons of her blouse.

"Get out," I said between clenched teeth, venom dripping from my tone.

Gage stood with a sigh. "Kayla, calm down. It's not —"

"Don't you dare tell me it's not what I think. Get this

bitch out of your office now."

A brewing storm darkened his expression, but I didn't care. I couldn't explain the fury roiling through me. Katherine had a way of getting under my skin. My jealousy manifested like a malignant tumor, reproducing bad cells faster than I could handle.

Katherine strutted toward me, hips swaying. "Piece of advice, Kayla. Men find jealous women unattractive."

She didn't know Gage at all, had no clue what made him tick. I did though, and I knew my jealousy fueled his desire for me. Maybe that's why I embraced the nasty emotion, rather than shove it below the surface. We fed off each other like wild animals. We fucked like wild animals too.

I wrenched the door open. "Don't presume to think you know shit about my husband or our relationship." I gestured to the doorway, ignoring the watchful eyes of the people on the fourth floor. "Get out."

She looked at Gage expectantly. "Are you going to let her treat the mother of your child like this?"

Gage parted his lips to speak, but I snapped my fingers in her face, bringing her attention to me again. "You might have popped his kid out, but I'm his wife. Conner is always welcome. You, on the other hand, are not."

She left in a huff, her overbearing perfume poisoning the air in her wake. I slammed the door and rounded on Gage.

"What the hell has gotten into you?" he shouted.

"Why was she here?"

"Shouldn't I be asking you that question? You think it's okay to barge into my office when you don't have permission to leave the damn house?"

"Fuck your permission, Gage." I jabbed a finger at his workspace. "What was she doing in your office, sitting on your *desk*? If you caught me in the same position, you'd go ballistic."

"Well that's the difference between you and me. I have reason to be jealous, don't I?"

Forget the elephant in the room; Ian stood like a brontosaurus.

"No more reason than I do," I said, willing my voice to remain steady. "The fact that you're refusing to answer is reason enough. You're fucking her, aren't you?"

He gritted his teeth. "We were talking about Conner. We'd almost reached an agreement on visitation when you stormed in and threw your tantrum."

"She needed to unbutton her shirt for that?"

He slammed his fist onto the desk. "Enough. I'm not doing this here. Go home and cool down." He rose, meaning to intimidate me with his full height.

Was he really not going to explain? The bastard expected me to return home to my prison, tail between my legs, and ignore how I'd found him in a compromising situation with another woman.

I folded my arms. "Her buttons, Gage." No way was I letting this go.

"You'd have to ask her," he said, rubbing his jaw, "seeing as how I paid her little attention. I was too busy going over the parenting plan." He came out from behind his desk. "Do you honestly think I notice anyone else? You're all I see, Kayla. How can you not know that?"

Because he wasn't all I saw. The truth washed over me like sour milk. The truth fucking reeked. I'd flirted with disaster, so maybe on a subconscious level, I expected him to as well. My gaze fell to the floor, and for the first time since finding her on his desk, I doubted my too-quick reaction.

"You have history with her." He had a *child* with her —a DNA connection he and I might never share.

"Are you kidding me?" He covered the distance between us. "My history with her means nothing. Not when I'm obsessed with fucking you into next week!" He clenched his hands, careful not to touch me. "You're behaving like a jealous adolescent. I mean it, Kayla. Go home."

I jutted my chin. "I'm tired of taking orders from you. This is bullshit," I said, swinging my hand in the air. "Have you ever heard of a courthouse? She has no business being in your office behind closed doors."

He grabbed my chin, applying enough pressure to make me back down. "I didn't want to punish you on the eve of our anniversary, but you're making that next to impossible."

"Don't kid yourself, Gage. Punishing me is the same as breathing for you."

"You want it? *Fine.*" He brought his face close to mine. "You've got it, baby. Go home and wait for me. If you're not on your knees in our bedroom, I'll give you more than my belt."

We faced off in a hushed battle for a few moments until Gage broke the standoff. He opened the door and waited for me to walk through it.

To submit to his orders.

My gaze lingered on his desk, remembering how her legs tempted just inches from his arm, how she'd unfastened her buttons to seduce him.

She was after my husband.

And I was a hypocrite because Ian was after me. I'd behaved no better than Gage. Worse, actually, because he wasn't attempting to hide her presence. He met with all sorts of people in this space—clients, PR people, financial advisors, employees of all levels. She was only one of many.

Afraid I was wearing my guilt on my face, I turned and fled.

12. THE TRUTH SHALL SET YOU ON FIRE

I returned home a half hour later, no calmer than when I'd left Channing Enterprises. His voice flitted through my mind, on constant loop. But instead of repeating what he'd said, my chaotic mind put words in his mouth, filling the holes of my insecurities with lies my heart believed were true—with things I was sure he hadn't had the guts to say.

If you hadn't interrupted, I would have fucked her on my desk.

You're just a slave, a toy I use for pleasure. She's the mother of my child. You can't compete with that.

I'll always be right, and you'll always be wrong.

Entering the bedroom, I let the door bang against the wall, and the nasty voice in my head changed his tune.

Do as you're told.

Don't argue.

Get on your knees.

On your knees, Kayla.

On your fucking knees now.

The sight of the floor set my teeth on edge. Hardwood, a means of torture for my joints, and he expected me to drop and wait until he decided to show his face. I tore across the room toward the bathroom, wondering if I were finally cracking. These past few weeks of sneaking around and stealing moments of freedom had finally caught up with me. This week alone had broken my spirit. Ian's reemergence into my life, the revelation of Conner's paternity, and the sexually frustrated nature Gage had left me in.

Going on autopilot in the bathroom, I stripped the clothes from my adrenaline-flushed body, dragged a brush through my wild hair. Prepared to become the slave he craved.

Always a slave.

Not a woman with feelings and wants and needs. My vision blurred with the hot sting of tears. The brush snagged on a tangle, and the dam finally broke.

Always crying, always bending, always taking the blame. He was right, and I was *always* wrong.

I glared at my reflection, hating the shell of a woman staring back. If he wanted to punish me, I'd give him a reason. Because blowing a gasket over finding another woman practically in his lap was a bullshit reason—an excuse to revel in his sadism at my expense. I'd done *nothing* wrong, unless I counted visiting sick children, eating lunch with a friend, and finding my husband with that...that *bitch*.

I yanked drawer after drawer open, contents rattling

under my fury. My pulse skyrocketed, then dived toward the ground at the sight of the red-handled shears. I reached a hand out but faltered.

He would be livid.

So what? Gage Channing would be mad. Big fucking deal. I grabbed the scissors and straightened my spine with purpose. Parting a thick section of hair, I counted to ten before raising the shears.

Snip.

The first lock of hair drifted to the tile. I brought the scissors to the left side of my head. Tears rimmed my eyes, threatening to spill over.

Snip. Snip. Snip.

My bare breasts heaved, nipples puckered. I didn't want to be warm. Warmth let feeling in, and I was suddenly and amazingly numb. Besides, warmth deceived with its inherent comfort, and comfort didn't exist in my world—not when he wanted me on my knees. Not when he wanted a meek and pliable and *obedient* robot for a wife.

Snip. Snip. Snip.

The severed strands circled my feet, freeing my shoulders from the weight of the red hair he loved so much. I couldn't help but recognize the significance in this moment, the symbolism, and it terrified me. It was only hair, but this rebellious act would change the tenuous dynamic we'd settled into for the past year. This very moment was about to fracture our world and expose the guts of our lies.

Narrowing my brows in determination, I faced the

reflection of the woman whose eyes lit up with something foreign. Something challenging.

Something he wouldn't like.

This strange woman from another time—before rules and rituals and Gage Fucking Channing—was reborn as she lifted the shears and cut off the last section of hair.

Movement in the mirror drew my attention. He stood in the open doorway behind me, his posture inflexible as always. My eyes swerved to his before dropping to the belt clasped in his determined fist.

I whirled, crossed my arms, and silently threw down a challenge. A belt wouldn't cut it this time. I knew it, and now he did too. No, on the eve of our first anniversary, Gage would have to do better than that.

"Do you mean to goad me?" he asked, flexing his hand around that strap of leather.

"What are you going to do about it? Lash me with your belt?" I grabbed the brush and yanked it through my newly cut hair. "Or maybe you'll have me sit on your desk next time, half dressed since you seem to enjoy that sort of thing." I raised a brow. "Huh, Gage? What are gonna do?"

He opened his mouth, shut it. Opened it again.

I blinked, feigning apathy, but I was shaking on the inside. He'd never looked so...at a loss. Unsure. After a year of submitting to his every order and whim, a single act of rebellion had knocked him on his sanctimonious ass. What a powerful, addicting feeling this was.

The belt slipped from his hand. "What do you want from me?" He spread his arms. "I've given you everything

—"

"No! I've given *you* everything." My voice rose. "I've spent more time on my knees than at your side. Have spent more time with your cock in my mouth than actually talking to you. You've forced your damn rules and jealous tirades on me, but I'm not allowed to feel anything when I see that bitch sitting on your desk like she fucking owns it?" I threw the hairbrush at him, but instead of hitting his face, it thumped against his broad chest. He caught it, folded his fingers around the handle, and I realized too late that I'd just given him a weapon.

He stalked into the bathroom, his body moving in a way that warned. I had no room to retreat, no way to defend myself as he grabbed my arm.

"Don't you dare judge me when you've been sneaking around for weeks working at *his* hospital."

I gasped, and the sails of my anger dropped, leaving me bobbing in a sea of blatant deception. Leaving me stagnant with guilt.

"That's right, Kayla." His gaze wandered my face, assessing the flush of guilt spreading across my cheeks. "I've known since you started." Letting go of my arm, he grabbed my chin, holding me prisoner in his furious indigo eyes. "Did you see him?"

"Yes." My admission crashed a wrecking ball through his heart, and my own fractured at the flicker of betrayal in his eyes. "Nothing happened. I ran into him a few days ago, and I told him to leave me alone."

"You really don't want to lie to me right now."

"Please, Gage. Don't do this."

His fingers slid from my jaw, and he fiddled with my short hair. "You started it, baby."

"I'm sorry." And I was. Not because I'd defied him. Not because I'd blown my top over Katherine. I was sorry because this was the worst time to poke at the frayed past named Ian Kaplan.

He lowered his eyes. "I've tried so hard not to come down on you about this. I've waited and waited and fucking waited for you to tell me."

The Friday ritual...I was right. He'd done it to punish me, maybe even to coax a confession out of me.

"I only wanted to do something meaningful with my spare time."

"You should have asked for permission."

"You would have said no."

He cocked his head. "You sound so sure of that."

"Are you saying you would have given your blessing?"

"That depends."

"On what?"

"On whether or not you're still in love with him."

For a few seconds, my lungs ceased working. The room and everything in it, including Gage, blurred, shifted. My eyes stung with the truth. I wasn't supposed to care about another man, especially when that man was his brother. I was certain my silence gave him all the answer he needed.

"Kayla..." he said, voice thick with pain. "What do you want from me? I've gone to counseling. I've been the best father I can be to Eve. I've worshipped the fucking ground you walk on, yet you go behind my—"

"You're slowly killing me!" I barreled past him and paced the bedroom, tired of being cornered, especially since he still held that brush with purpose. "Your love is toxic. I can't fucking breathe anymore."

Spanning the distance, he held my left hand and ran his thumb over my wedding ring. The one that meant so much to him because it had belonged to his mother. "I've given you everything I can. Everything that I am."

"You don't get it!" I yanked my hand from his. "I need more than this. I need to be able to walk out the door when I want. See who I want. Wear what I want. Get a damn job if I want."

"Then explain it to me. Why do you need those things?"

I blinked several times. That was not the reaction I'd expected. "Because...because I just do." I brought my fist to my chest. "I need a piece of *me* back."

In the space of two seconds, he had my chin in his strong grip. "But you gave every piece of yourself to me the day we married. I need you to submit, always."

Like a flash going off behind my eyes, it all became devastatingly clear. Control. It would always whittle down to his thirst for complete control over every aspect of his life, and now mine. He'd had none growing up. I'd known this, and maybe I'd understood it on a subconscious level. I'd bent for him for a year because I'd wanted to make him happy—because giving him everything meant giving him the security he needed.

"The question goes both ways, Gage. Why do you need it?" I wondered if he'd figured out what I had, or if it was still a need that chewed inside him, mostly uncategorized.

His forehead creased. His eyes narrowed. He struggled to speak.

"You don't know why you need it, do you?"

"You're asking me to change who I am. I can't, Kayla. I've already bended the most I can bend."

"No, I've bended. Every damn day, I've given up myself for your needs."

"You're more limber than I am, baby."

"Don't joke about this."

"It's not a joke. You're the strongest woman I know. Nothing can break you, not even me. You're my miracle."

"I shouldn't have to be so strong."

"But you are." He held my gaze with meaning. Paused a beat. "Only you can handle what I need." He tapped the hairbrush against his palm. "And what I need right now is to blister your ass."

"Just when I think we're getting somewhere." I yanked at my infinity collar, brimming with restless energy —a tonic of anger, desperation, and even regret. "Take it off, Gage. I'm done handling your shit."

He struck so fast, I didn't have time to gasp. I dangled over his shoulder, the hardwood floor of our bedroom my only view as he stalked toward the bed.

"Let me go!"

He dropped me to my feet and forced me over the end. "Ass up, Kayla."

I kicked and yelled and slung obscenities at him.

"Knock it off. Take your punishment like a fucking

adult."

"Why should I, when you treat me like a child?"

"If you don't behave, I'll make you wish you had."

"Let. Me. Go."

"Do you remember your wedding vows, or do you need a reminder?"

"Do you?" I fired back.

He smacked my ass with such strength, the world seemed to halt. I cried out, my eyes stinging, muscles rigid from the fiery imprint of his hand. That hairbrush was going to be torture in comparison. I held to no delusions; he had every intention of beating me with it. The thought stole my breath, and I fought for air until my lungs filled. The world jerked forward, returning to its laborious orbit around the sun.

Just like I would. I'd orbit Gage because he was that powerful. He was the center of my solar system, the God of my gravity, the devil of my desire. The Master of my mind.

He was the dean of my discipline.

"Let's try this again," he said, squeezing where his palm had just put me in line. "Do you remember your vows?"

"Yes! Of course I do."

"I want to hear them. One at a time." He shifted and stood to the side. With ceremonial significance, he placed the brush on the mattress in front of me. Fisting a hand in my shortened locks, he forced my gaze on his chosen implement of punishment.

Wooden, square, made durable for long hair...which I

no longer had.

Warm fingers skimmed the back of my thighs, inching my skirt up to expose his naked canvas. "You're getting five strikes for each vow, but for each one you've broken, you're getting twenty-five." He released his grip on my hair and picked up the brush again. "Don't plan to sit anytime soon."

I wanted to scream at him. Wanted to tell him to go screw himself. But he had me right where he wanted me, and I knew from experience that the only way out was to follow his orders.

"Okay, Gage. You win."

Whack.

"Ahhh!"

"Address me properly."

"I'm sorry, Master."

"Start reciting."

"I promised to love."

"Love me, you have. I know I'm difficult to love, but I feel the way you love me every time you drop to your knees."

Whack.

"Every time you make yourself gag so I'll come that much harder."

Whack.

"Every time you take my belt."

Whack.

"Every time you've let me kiss your tears away."

Whack.

"Every time you come with my name on your lips."

Whack.

"Every time you watch me with Eve." Dead silence followed his words. He cleared his throat. "You don't realize that I'm paying attention, but I am, Kayla. I see the amazing smile that lights up your face. Your joy is a fucking weapon." He drew in a shaky breath. "Next vow."

I couldn't breathe, couldn't see through my tears, so I wasn't sure how he expected me to speak. But that didn't matter. I'd better find a way to utter what he wanted to hear, or face even harsher consequences.

"To honor."

"Have you, Kayla? Have you honored me?"

If I were being truthful… "No, Master. But you haven't honored me either."

"How do you figure? You've been sneaking behind my back for weeks. How have I dishonored you?"

I figured now wasn't the time to bring up the double standard—the fact that he'd hid something from me as well. But there were no double standards with Gage. Only my obedience.

"You don't respect me," I said. "You don't care how I feel. You'll always do what you want, and what I want doesn't matter."

"You're right. I will do what I want, but that doesn't mean you don't matter. You matter more than you realize. I've made concessions I didn't think I was capable of making. I stood by knowing you were seeing him, and I said *nothing.*"

God, he was right. I had no argument to stand on.

"We'll call this one a draw," he said. "Next vow." The

tone of his voice dipped to a dangerous level.

We both knew what was coming. His triumph over punishing me, and my struggle to endure it because I had broken the last vow. I'd stood on that altar and promised to obey him. It didn't matter that his expectations and demands were beyond fucked up—I'd married him with both eyes open.

He hadn't changed. He'd remained his usual volatile yet ironically dependable self. If I could count on anything, it was that Gage Channing would *always* punish me.

"Obey," I whispered.

"Did you break that vow?"

The words wouldn't come at first. A lifetime seemed to go by in the time it took to force out the answer he thirsted for. "Yes, Master."

"Yes, you did. Even worse, you broke my cold as fuck heart." He brought the brush down with maximum strength, stealing the essence of my life-force. My lungs refused to work. My muscles refused to relax and take the strike. My brain's synapses were stuck firing down a one-way street. The boulevard of broken man. Gage had a heart—fragile and infested with love for me.

I'd stomped on it by not giving him all of mine.

"You could have volunteered anywhere. Any goddamn fucking place, Kayla. But you chose *that* hospital. Why?"

"I don't know," I cried, not even flinching when he hit me again.

"Yes, you do. You just don't want to admit it."

Whack.

"Fuck, Kayla, out of every man on this planet for you to be in love with, why'd it have to be him?"

My body quaked from the force of his words.

"I love you more." I shuttered my eyes, too ashamed to look at him because my non-denial spoke volumes. I was in love with two men. To finally admit and accept it shredded my soul. "Forgive me, Master."

I glanced over my shoulder, and for the second time ever, I watched him struggle to hold it together. Tears hinged on dark, thick lashes. He blinked rapidly, each drop purging him of turmoil and grief and heartbreak.

"I'll die trying, Kayla." He lifted the brush, and my ass became the devil's playground.

13. FOUR MINUTES PAST MIDNIGHT

This was the worst way to start off our anniversary trip. We'd pulled ourselves together long enough to welcome Eve off the bus and get her ready for when Leah's mother picked her up for the sleepover.

But we'd barely said two words to each other since we'd loaded our bags into the trunk over an hour ago. I shifted in my seat, hissing between my teeth because no matter how I moved, I couldn't escape the pain from the force of that brush.

He'd walloped my ass good.

I shot him a sideways glance. A shadow darkened his jawline. I imagined a dark cloud obscured his eyes as well.

"How many times did you see him?" His question filled up the festering space, piercing my ears louder than the highway rushing beneath us.

"I met with him once," I said then lowered my voice. "Ran into him twice after that."

He gripped the steering wheel as if the thing threatened to break off and roll away. "Did you *run* into him on purpose?"

"No, Gage. It wasn't on my end."

"Address me properly."

I sighed. This was getting us nowhere.

"I mean it, Kayla. Address me properly, or I'll pull the car over." He threw me a look full of devious meaning. "After what I put your ass through earlier, trust me—you don't want more."

"Yes, Master."

"Did he touch you?"

Shit. He wasn't about to let this go any more than I'd been willing to let him off the hook about Katherine and her undone buttons. I recalled how Ian had grabbed my hand, how he'd trapped me between him and the couch. How he'd kissed me for the merest of seconds.

All of those things would jab at Gage's anger.

"Just tell me the truth, Kayla. Don't overthink it."

"He touched me," I admitted quietly.

"How?"

"Grabbed my hand, mostly."

His Adam's apple bobbed in this throat. "Did you touch him?"

"Only to push him away."

His jaw was so rigid, I wondered if it would split in two.

The remainder of the drive went by in utter disquiet. Gage focused his attention on getting us safely over the worst part of the snowy pass. By the time we pulled into the driveway of a secluded cabin, nightfall had descended hours ago. Fluffy, white snow weighed down the surrounding pine trees, and the inches on the rooftop must have reached a foot or more.

I opened my door, grateful that someone had plowed the driveway and cleared a path to the front door. My boots crunched on packed-down snow, fracturing the cold serenity of winter. Gage popped the trunk, hefted a suitcase and a duffle out, and gestured for me to precede him to the stoop.

"It's beautiful out here," I said.

"It's secluded. I had to pay a premium to get someone out here to ready the place for us. No one's around for miles." We reached the front door, and the way his gaze lingered on me sent nervous flutters into my belly.

"For two days, it's just you and me, Kayla."

Just the two of us...and me at his mercy. Eve wouldn't provide a buffer between us. His work wouldn't save me with a well-timed distraction. Being in the middle of nowhere with him was nerve-wracking enough on its own, but considering how hurt and furious he was...

He set the luggage down long enough to unlock the door. I entered first, and a blast of warmth hit me. A fire raged in the insert. The plush throw rug in front of the flames would be the perfect spot to make love all night.

The thought squeezed my heart. I missed making love with him. These past few weeks, he'd been more dominant than loving.

He dropped our luggage by the front entrance. "No TV, no distractions. I'd planned to make you come all weekend until you begged me to stop."

Past tense.

Forget making love by the fireplace. I'd ruined this weekend and any chance of that happening.

No, a logical voice in my head piped in. We'd ruined the weekend. I'd been in the wrong, but he wasn't innocent either. He should have never allowed Katherine inside his office, let alone plant her ass on his desk.

He dragged a hand through his hair. "I want you naked, now."

Blinking several times, I held it all in, refused to fall apart. But the way he was acting stabbed at my hurt, opening old wounds. I couldn't take it when he grew cold and distant. I could take just about anything but that.

"Yes, Master," I choked out, shrugging out of my coat. I reached for the hem of my sweater, but his warm palm on my cheek stopped me. He leaned down and took my mouth. The slow slide of his tongue against mine melted all my doubts, all my fears.

The tears finally broke free, streaming down my cheeks, dampening the stubble on his face. Cleansing us. I clutched his jacket, needing his reassurance more than ever.

"I'm sorry, Master," I said with a gasp.

"Shhh." His command feathered across my well-kissed lips. "I know, baby." The low, sexy tenor of his voice hit me in places where I was most vulnerable. Right at the center of my heart and between my thighs.

"Get naked for me, then go lie down on your stomach on the rug." He pointed toward the fireplace. "I'll put our bags in the bedroom."

Less than five minutes later, he had me sprawled by

the fire. The rhythmic movement of his hands as he rubbed lotion into my skin cast me under a curious spell —one where the pain from the hairbrush ceased. But his gentleness also widened the crack in my spirit, until every last bit of sorrow and regret gushed from me in a torrential downpour. As I replayed my punishment, in which he'd extracted each vow, I wasn't sure if I hurt for him or for me.

He said I'd broken his heart.

"I'm in love with *you*." My voice hitched on a sob.

"I know." He hovered over my back and pressed his lips to my shoulder. "I never doubted that, Kayla."

"I never meant to hurt you." My diaphragm spasmed with a hiccup.

"I know that as well." He scooted down my body, placing kisses along my spine, and his breath heated the small of my back. Gentle fingers kneaded my stinging flesh. Then he ran a finger between my ass cheeks and stalled at my puckered hole.

"Are you done punishing me?" I tensed, waiting for his next move. The simple act of him teasing my asshole made me nervous.

"I'll never tire of punishing you." He rolled me to my back and gently wedged my thighs apart. "Every Friday night until the day I die."

So the ritual was permanent. For the rest of my life, I'd endure his belt. Just because.

Because that's who he was.

"What if I don't want that?"

He crawled up my body and grasped my hair. "As

long as you're my wife, you'll get my belt." He nipped at my neck, right above the collar. "But you'll also get me, Kayla. Every part of me. You have my fucking soul."

"Not every part of you," I pointed out.

"What do you mean?"

"I want your control."

"So we're back to that, are we?"

Wood crackled in the fireplace, drawing my attention. The clock above the mantel ticked.

Tick, tick, tick.

Each second brought us closer to our anniversary when the shackles on my orgasms would unlock and fall to the ground.

"That was the agreement. I make it to our anniversary, you give me what I want." I gestured toward the clock. "Our anniversary begins in fifteen minutes."

I expected worry to darken his features. Maybe even resignation. Anything but the devilish grin that widened his mouth.

"Guess that means I've got fifteen minutes to make you come."

As he lowered his head between my thighs, I became dizzy with delirium. It seemed like weeks instead of days since he'd gone down on me. His warm breath hit my aching core an instant before his mouth did. And he didn't start off slow. Instead of teasing, like he'd been doing for days, he flattened his tongue on my clit and added the perfect amount of pressure.

My spine arched, and I moaned deep in my throat, seconds away from coming undone. My fingers found their way into his hair and clutched him to me. Begged me to push him away. What a dilemma.

I dug my heels into the rug, pushed up on my elbows, and tried to scoot out of reach. His hold on me tightened. Upon my frustrated cry, he raised his head and ensnared me inside blue eyes full of cunning design.

"Don't move." His do-as-I-say-or-else tone put an end to the fight in my bones. I froze, my gaze prisoner to his.

"That's better." Letting go of one hip, he slowly dipped a finger into my pussy, watching me the whole time. Studying my reaction. Calculating how far he'd have to go to push me over the edge before midnight. "You're going to come on my tongue, whether you want to or not."

"If I don't, will you honor our agreement?"

Rubbing his rough cheek against my inner thigh, he smiled—just a tiny curve of his lips, but I saw it.

"You'll come." He sounded way too confident as he thrust another finger inside me, and I wondered if he wasn't right. "Don't move," he warned again before returning his mouth to my clit and moving his tongue in a steady back and forth rhythm. My head plopped to the floor, and a soundless breath escaped.

Back and forth, up and down.

Flick, flick, flick.

Pressure...God, the pressure. I was nothing but a throbbing bundle of nerves between my legs.

I clenched my fists at my sides and willed myself not to move. Not to push my mound more firmly into his mouth. Not to let the upsurge of release burst through my faulty barricade.

Because I wanted him underneath me, tied to the bed, his mouth gagged. I wanted him at my mercy, only this time, I wanted to have none.

I wanted to unleash my demons and watch them rain down on him.

But hell, if he kept this up, I had no doubt he'd make me come before midnight. I cast a glance at the clock. Eight more minutes. Seemed like forever. I fastened my attention on that slow moving hand as it taunted with its lazy jaunt through each number. Zeroed in on the constant *tick, tick, tick* that kept perfect timing with his expertly timed tongue.

"Eyes on me."

He would allow me no distractions. No way out. But he couldn't command my thoughts. He couldn't read my mind, so I mentally counted the ticks.

One…two…three…four…

His finger brought me back with a devious crook, pressing *that spot* just right. I launched his name from my lips with a painful groan.

"Who am I, Kayla?"

"Master," I choked.

Counting…

God, where was I?

Eight…nine…ten…eleven…

Another come-hither crook. Another concentration break. I whimpered for more, even as I relaxed my muscles and hurtled every thought and feeling away from the rush of heat building in me.

Away from his vicious tongue.

"That's right, baby. Come for me. You know you want to."

I squeezed my eyes shut. "No…please. Stop!"

Another flick of his tongue, followed by a snicker. "You're drenched. There's no stopping this, so let go. Come on my tongue."

He went in for the kill, intending to rocket me into deep space. I shook my head, chanted *no, no, no* in time with the incessant ticking that brought me one second closer to freedom.

The freedom to jump off the ledge. God knew I clung to it until the last possible second. Cried in disappointed anguish as his lips and tongue and devious fingers sent me plummeting head first.

Spiraling.

Screaming.

Shattering.

"Gage…" I held on to his head for the ride, squirming underneath him, back arching. Mouth gaping.

His triumphant moan vibrated to my core, making me claw at his shoulders.

"Oh God!" A week of denial had primed me for the ultimate surrender, and another body spasm bent me to his will. I succumbed to his tongue with everything I had, turned to lava, flooded his greedy mouth.

More.

There was only more.

By the time I slammed back to Earth, my body

drenched in sweat and utterly spent, I was malleable flesh in his hands. Easy prey. Too susceptible to his guile.

He almost had me—had almost obliterated me beyond thought or reason. But I remembered to glance at the clock, and a slow grin stretched across my face. "It's four minutes past midnight."

His gaze swerved to the instrument that would ultimately be his downfall, because I had no intention of letting him get out of this.

"So it seems," he said with a frown.

"I want your control."

He shot a hand out and squeezed my nipple. "I'm still your Master. Don't forget that."

"Please, Master?" I fluttered my lashes at him.

He shook his head with a sigh, but something about the way his mouth twitched gave me hope. He almost seemed…amused. Last year, he hadn't believed I had it in me, and he'd been right. I'd tested the waters of making him submit, but I hadn't gone after it with purpose. With absolute bravery.

With the obsession that ran through my veins now.

A year had twisted my psyche into something beyond innocent. Not only did I want to watch him writhe, but I wanted payback.

"A deal's a deal," he said.

My pulse thrummed in anticipation.

"Under one condition."

Of course there was a condition. Gage specialized in the language of contingencies.

"What do you want, Master?"

"I want you to remove anal as a hard limit. Give me your tight little ass whenever I please, and I'll give you what you want for *one* night."

"That doesn't sound fair. How about a night of anal for a night of your submission?" I countered.

"You're lucky I'm negotiating at all. I can do what I want, whenever I want. That's what owning you means, Kayla. That's what it means to be a slave. You yield to me —not the other way around."

"Why are we having this discussion then? Take what you want. Force me. Hold me down and show me what it means to be a man." My voice rattled with scorn. "Hurt me. Make me cry. Is that what you want?" I was on the verge of tears again.

Something in my tone must have gotten through to him. The severity of his expression softened. "I want you to give it to me." He slid a hand under my ass and teased the spot he was dying to penetrate. "Don't make me force you."

"Don't make me beg you not to."

He dropped his head between my thighs, his sigh of concession a feather on my skin. "Remove the hard limit. In return I'll give you what you want every year on our anniversary."

It was more than I could have hoped for. More than I thought he'd ever give.

"Promise?"

"I swear on my love for you."

"Will you be gentle?" He'd been gentle in Vegas, but I sensed a restless energy in him that scared me.

"Always."

I chewed on it for a few moments, bottom lip pulled between my teeth, and nodded.

"Since we're laying our cards on the table," he said, bracing himself above me on his forearms, "your volunteer work at his hospital is ceasing *yesterday*. Do you understand me?"

"Gage—"

"Don't even think about arguing with me."

I clamped my mouth shut.

"You may volunteer at any damn place you want, but if you ever set foot in that hospital again, or talk to him, or touch him, you will *not* like the consequences." He grabbed my chin with the harshness of the pre-marriage Gage, who was not only a controlling and sadistic bastard, but a psychotic, controlling, and sadistic bastard.

There was definitely a difference.

"I don't share, least of all with him," he said. "Are we clear?"

I nodded, my throat too constricted to speak.

"Good. Now enough of this bullshit. My cock is in desperate need of your mouth." He climbed to his knees, unbuttoned and lowered his zipper, then moved to perch on my chest. Prepared to *take*.

I shot a hand out and placed it against his abs. "You said a deal's a deal. It's our anniversary, so I believe it's my turn to call the shots."

He dropped his head with a laugh. "You wicked, wicked woman. You might have the world fooled with those I'm-innocent eyes, but I'm on to you."

I veered upright and shoved him back. He dropped to his haunches, his dark hair a sexy, disheveled masterpiece. I rose to my feet and crossed to where he'd set a single duffle bag next to the couch.

Gage's bag of tricks.

For the next 24 hours, it would be *my* bag of tricks. I felt his attention on my back as I unzipped it. Glancing over my shoulder, I found him in the position I'd left him.

"I'm going to miss that hair," he said. "But I've got to admit the short length is not without merit. You're gorgeous no matter what you do."

My fingers caressed a buckle. "Are you trying to sweet talk me, Mr. Channing?"

"Maybe just a little, Mrs. Channing."

Spending time with him like this—with the air full of laughter and love and happiness—was amazing. As I pulled the cuffs from the bag, I realized how harrowing our lives had become. But maybe that was the cost of harboring such intense passion. We felt things deeply. Loved with depth, lusted with insanity, angered with the burn of an inferno, hurt with the force of a blast.

We were both a little insane.

I carried the cuffs to him, but instead of restraining his wrists, I dropped to my knees and let them crash to the floor. I launched myself at him, much like I had the first time I'd gone to him of my own accord, free of coercion. My hands ended up in his hair, our mouths melded together, and his arms circled my waist, pulling me closer. I wasn't sure who was submitting—seemed like we both were.

We were submitting to something bigger than the two of us.

"Do I have to call you Mistress?" He was nowhere near taking this seriously.

"I don't care what you call me, as long as you get naked and let me cuff you to the bed." I rose, picked up the restraints, and sauntered toward the bedroom, not bothering to see if he would follow.

I knew he would.

14. KAYLA'S REWARD

Gage lay spread-eagled on the bed, his wrists and ankles trapped inside his own cuffs. I'd buckled those fuckers tight. He wasn't getting free. The way he followed my movements with his nervous gaze told me that he knew it too.

Digging through our suitcase, I selected one of his silk ties—a deep blue color that brought out the brightness of his eyes—and climbed over his powerful abs to straddle him.

"Lift your head," I told him.

"You're having too much fun with this."

"You have no idea."

"Did you forget who you're talking to?" He raised his head off the mattress by a couple of inches. "I know you better than you know yourself. You've hungered for this."

"You're right, I have. Now shut up." I fastened the tie around his eyes. "No talking unless you're begging."

He pressed his lips together, but a devious curve hinted at a smile. I scraped my fingernails down his chest, enjoying how his muscles jumped under my touch, and hunched between his muscular thighs.

His cock was huge, harder than the man himself. I wet my lips, my pulse racing in my ears as I hovered. Waited. Drew out the torture. I lowered my mouth over the tip, and he balled his hands, rattling the chains tethering him to the four poster bed. I'd barely touched him, but he was already squirming.

God, I loved this power.

He could hold off for hours when he was in control, but take control away from the sadist, and he came undone at the slightest provocation.

I fondled his tight balls as I swirled my tongue. He raised his hips, bringing his cock deeper into my mouth. I squeezed his sack and clamped down with my teeth, not enough to hurt, but enough to tame him.

"Fuck, Kayla."

"I don't hear you begging yet. Are you allowed to speak unless you're begging?" He didn't answer, so I increased the pressure on his testicles. "Answer me. Are you allowed to speak?"

"No!"

"That's right, my sexy husband. I don't want to hear it unless you're ready to admit defeat. I want your surrender." I ran my tongue along the length of his shaft, from base to head.

"Baby, take me in." He raised his hips again, seeking entrance into my mouth. I flicked the slit at the end, and he sucked a painful breath between clenched teeth.

"I'm in charge," I reminded him. "You don't get to

shove your cock into my mouth. You'll get what I give you when I give it to you."

"You've learned too fucking much from me."

"You're the best teacher, Gage. Just think of all the things I'll pick up before our next anniversary."

He groaned. "Giving in to you was a bad idea."

"I disagree," I whispered, licking and tasting. "I love this idea." I softened my lips and sucked on his tip, flicking my tongue back and forth. Keeping my eyes on him, I glorified in the sweat that broke out on his temples as I bobbed my mouth on and off his shaft.

Just the head of it.

Just enough to get his blood pumping.

Gage would hold onto his last thread of control until I wrenched it from his being. And I wasn't fooled—taking him there would require some work.

Steady, patient work. My mouth had a long road ahead of it. I let my eyes drift shut and gave myself over to the heady taste of him on my tongue, to the sensation of his silky soft tip sliding between my lips.

Tonight, I owned his cock, and I could kiss it for as long as I wanted. Tease it for as long as I wanted. Torture it for as long as I wanted.

I *wanted*.

"Good God, you're killing me." He lifted his hips again, and I gave his sack another squeeze.

"You're not behaving. Don't make me punish you."

That drew a laugh from him. "I'd like to see you try."

Letting go of his balls, I sucked on my finger before inching it up his ass.

He howled, a cross between pain and intense arousal. Taking advantage of his helplessness, I pulled his entire length into my mouth and gagged.

"Shit," he groaned. "Take my cock down your throat." He pulled at the restraints, his spine arching, his lips imparting groan after groan. Every muscle in his body had turned on him, holding him captive to my torture.

I had him.

For the first time ever, I had him.

"Dammit, Kayla. Give me your mouth. Stop fucking around."

"Is your cock throbbing for me?"

He growled. "You know it is."

Grinning like a true sadist, I took him in my mouth and drew his shaft down my throat like I meant it. He veered upward like a man possessed. I circled the base with one hand and kept time with my busy mouth as my finger played with his ass.

And I took him there—that tricky place where one more slide of my lips would send him spinning out of control.

"God, yes…oh fuck…don't you dare stop."

Abruptly, I pulled away.

"Kayla, for God's sake, make me come."

"Maybe in a few hours."

"Baby, I need you. It's been too fucking long."

"What you need doesn't matter tonight. You're not coming until I say so." A wicked grin captured my lips. "I can make you edge all night long."

He groaned, thrashing his head back and forth, and wrenched at the restraints with real effort, as if determined to break free from the metal chains keeping him at my mercy.

"You'd better make me come long and hard before you unlock me."

"You think you deserve to come?"

"I think you're going to *want* me to come."

"Why would I want that?"

"I promised I'd be gentle with your ass." He licked his lips. "If you don't fuck me like you mean it, I won't be held responsible for my actions."

Oh, boy.

If he kept talking like that, I might lose my nerve. I scrambled from the bed and returned to the bag of tricks I'd dropped on the floor inside the door of the bedroom. Digging through the various implements of torture and pleasure, I settled on a solid rubber ball gag. I also grabbed a flogger. For some reason, approaching him with these foreign items in my hands made me question my ability to go through with this.

Don't back down now. Do it right or don't do it at all.

Sitting astride his chest, I pushed the rubber ball to his lips. "Open your mouth."

"Jeez, Kayla."

Shifting positions, so I was able to reach his cock, I gripped the handle of the flogger and brought it down on his throbbing, wet tip. He cried out in shock, every muscle in his body spasming.

"Take the gag, or I'll keep striking your prized

possession."

"You're my prized possession."

"Open your mouth," I demanded, pressing the gag to his lips once more.

He fought me for a while until the fifth strike landed with the kind of force that drew a high-pitched cry from him. Breathing hard, he gave in and parted his lips. I wound the strap around his head and fastened the buckle, my pulse skittering at my throat.

He was mine.

Unable to move.

Unable to break free.

His eyesight taken.

His voice silenced.

With a sigh of satisfaction, I mounted him and positioned myself over his erection, holding shy of his tip for thirty seconds before taking him deep inside, inch by slow inch.

He moaned, writhed underneath me, his body a powerful machine disarmed by my longing to conquer. His hips took over, held hostage by his current state of mind. They wouldn't stop thrusting. Right when I sensed him teetering on the edge of orgasm, I jerked up and let his cock slip free. The gag made anything he said unintelligible, but I was positive he slung muffled obscenities at me.

This was going to be hell for him and heaven for me. I counted to sixty, one palm pressed against his chest where his heartbeat thundered, then I sank onto his cock again and rode him to the next edge.

And the next.

There were an infinite amount of edges on this night when time ceased to exist. I let my head tilt back, my short hair brushing the back of my shoulders, and rolled my nipples between two fingers.

"Do you want to know what I'm doing right now?"

I took his stifled moan as a yes.

"I'm playing with my nipples. Pinching them hard, Gage." Taking control from him was empowering. Exhilarating. I could do this until the sun rose.

But two hours later, my resolve wavered. Sweat drenched us both. I'd ridden him slow and steady the whole time, pulling off whenever he came close to blowing his load. But I was getting antsy. I wanted to feel his lips under mine, our tongues clashing together in mutual madness, and when I came again, I wanted him to take the plunge with me.

If that made me weak, then so be it. I found more satisfaction in pleasuring him than hurting him. Leaning forward, I unbuckled the gag and tossed it on the floor.

"You're in deep shit, Kayla."

"Shh," I said, placing a finger against his mouth. His ragged breaths puffed against my skin. "Don't make me put the gag back in."

"I hope you enjoy a red ass."

"I'm only doing what you gave me permission to do." I removed the tie and watched him blink me into focus. His deep blue eyes trapped me, dragged me under. I was sitting astride him while he couldn't move, but I was the one submitting now.

With a quick thrust of my hips, I impaled myself.

"Fuuuuck…" He bucked, angling up to meet me. "You're so fucking beautiful."

I whimpered, my mouth colliding with his, and our tongues tangled as we joined in a new tempo.

The dance of languid fluidity.

"So fucking good," he rasped. "You want control? Take it. I'm all yours."

"What will you do if I untie you?"

"Do it and find out."

Deliberating between having him exactly where I wanted him, and being exactly where I wanted to be, I ran my fingers along his bicep. "If I release you, no anal."

"I can't promise that."

"I don't mean *ever*, I just mean tonight." I bit my lip. "I want something else, Gage."

"You're a demanding little thing tonight, aren't you?"

Bringing my lips to his, barely touching, breathing him in, I worked on unbuckling his left wrist. "I don't want chains, cuffs, whips, or clamps. I just want you."

"You have me," he said, threading his fingers through my hair. "I'm at your fucking mercy."

"Then love me."

"I do love you. So damn much."

"That's not what I meant. You used to make love to me, but lately, all you do is fuck me."

Licking his lips, he pulled on the restraint trapping his right hand. "Let me go."

I studied him, uncertainty straining my mouth.

"Baby, trust me."

"I do trust you," I whispered as I released his right wrist, followed by his ankles. He hauled me into his arms and flipped us.

Hands in my hair.

Mouth coaxing mine open so his could plunder.

He slipped inside me with the sort of patience I didn't expect. The weight of his body grew heavy. Each thrust wrenched synchronized howls from us, his a heated blast on my neck, and mine unleashed into the air as I arched underneath him, head thrown back. He laced our fingers together and shoved my hands to the mattress.

It had been so long since he'd done more than take; tonight, he gave something priceless in return. Gave a little piece of himself in the way he held me, the way he kissed me, the way he surrendered even though I was on my back again with my hands pressed to the bed.

Mostly, the unhindered loss of control strangling his vocal cords was the real gift. "You feel so fucking good. I can't stand it." He jerked to a halt. "So good. Come with me."

With a breathless cry, I followed him over the edge.

15. ULTIMATE SIN

I lived off the high of that night and Gage's submission for three weeks straight. That weekend had been a tipping point for us, and we fell into a new routine of sorts. Friday night still came around like clockwork, but something had finally settled, finding its rightful place in the midst of our marriage.

Our anniversary and the unveiling of my deception had helped us build a new foundation.

But with new beginnings came new endings. I hadn't been allowed to visit Emma at all, despite begging him for the privilege. I had many freedoms I hadn't had before our anniversary meltdown and reconstruction, but he wouldn't budge on the subject of Ian or anything about Ian.

Sadly, that included what he referred to as *his hospital.*

A rare occurrence of blue skies and sunshine made the day perfect for running errands. A nippy breeze rustled my hair as I unlocked the front door. I hefted a bag of groceries in one arm and pushed my way inside.

My phone went off in my pocket on the way to the kitchen. I set the bag on the counter and dug out my cell, finding Simone's smiling face flashing on the screen.

"Hey, what's up?" I held the phone between my shoulder and ear so I could unload the bag of groceries.

"Kayla," she said, her tone immediately putting me on alert.

I halted, and a jar of spaghetti sauce thudded on the counter. "What's wrong? Is Emma okay?"

"Emma's fine. Great actually. She's going home in about another week."

I let out a relieved breath. "That's great to hear."

"It is." She paused. "I didn't call about Emma though. Can we meet somewhere to talk?"

I glanced at the time on the microwave. Gage had given me four hours to do my errands. I still had an hour left. "Of course. Where should I meet you?"

"Can you come to the hospital?"

I hesitated. "I haven't eaten lunch yet. That pizza place a few blocks away sounds good. You up for that?"

She sighed. "Don't bullshit me, Kayla."

"I can't meet you at the hospital. I'm sorry."

"The pizza place it is then. See you in twenty." She hung up, and I stared at my cell for a few moments, bewildered. Something was wrong. She was never that curt, even for Simone.

I rushed to put the groceries away, checked for any new messages from Gage, then hurried out the door. Traffic was heavier than usual, causing me to walk into the pizza place ten minutes late.

Simone sat in a booth by herself. "I ordered pepperoni," she said.

"Okay." I slid in across from her, studying her distraught face. Fear tightened my gut. "You're worrying me. What's going on?"

She wouldn't quite look at me, and when she wiped a tear away, I reached out and grabbed her hand.

"He needs you right now," she said, holding onto my fingers like a lifeline.

"Who?" I squeezed her hand back, wishing my ears would rebel and not listen. There was only one *he* she could be referring to.

"He came looking for you a couple of weeks ago. I told him you'd quit your job, and things just…happened. We started having lunch together every day."

"Okay…" I eyed her cautiously, wondering where she was going with this. As much as it hurt to think of Ian with anyone, I wanted him to be happy. I also wanted Simone to be happy, so if they were hitting it off… "If you guys are dating, I think that's…it's great, Simone."

"We're not dating. I've grown attached, but we're not dating." She chewed on her bottom lip. "He didn't want me to tell you, but I can't keep my mouth shut on this. Kayla, he's sick."

"Sick?" Like with the flu or bronchitis or pneumonia. As I swept my bangs to the side, the tremor in my fingers said otherwise. That tremor knew the truth before she said it.

"He's got cancer."

I shook my head, denying. "But I just saw him three

weeks ago. He was fine."

"He's far from fine," she snapped. "He hasn't been to work in days. He's stopped treatment. I think he's given up." Another tear slipped down her cheek. "You need to talk to him. He's still in love with you. Maybe he'll listen to you because I can't get through his thick skull."

"What are his chances?" I blinked, willing my eyes to stay dry. If I started crying, I wouldn't stop, and that wouldn't help anyone.

"Without treatment?" She dropped her head. "Not good."

Our order arrived then. The waitress set the steaming pizza between us, but neither of us had an appetite.

I didn't want to believe her, and I knew part of me would refuse to accept it until I heard it from him. I stood, glanced around the restaurant at the half-filled booths, the people from the nearby hospital and other businesses gathering to share lunch. The setting appeared too normal. Just another day. I wanted to scream at everyone and ask how they could go about their day as the earth shook under my feet. It all seemed so unfair.

"Do you have his address?"

She pulled a pen from her purse and wrote on a napkin before pushing it into my hands. "You'll talk to him?" Hope held her vocal cords captive.

I clutched his address to my chest. "I'll try."

"Get him to start the chemo again. We both know how fast things can turn around. He's throwing away any chance he has of living."

It was true. Volunteering in the oncology wing had

taught me a lot, and Simone had more firsthand experience with this frail thing called life than I did. Fear seized my gut. Eve had come close to dying, and she would have if Gage hadn't intervened. People could definitely take a turn for the better with the right treatment…but it didn't always play out like that.

"I'll talk to him." Vomit had found a new home in my throat. Simone and I exchanged one last glance before I exited the restaurant in a fog and slid behind the wheel of the shiny Lexus Gage had bought for me. I wasn't sure how I'd gotten to the car, or how I made it to the other side of the Willamette River.

I pulled into his driveway, or at least, what I believed to be his driveway. The parking spots were empty, so unless he'd parked his SUV in the garage, he either wasn't home, or I'd found the wrong place. I exited the car, cringing when the slam of the driver's side door ricocheted in the quiet, and headed toward the front door.

Stepping onto his stoop, I raised my hand, readying myself to knock, and almost turned around. Simone had to be wrong. Ian was fine. He'd seemed perfectly healthy three weeks ago, if not a little…off. Swallowing my fear, I pounded on the door. Footsteps sounded from the other side. Something crashed, a curse whispered through the door, then the lock clicked over before he yanked open the barrier standing between us.

My knees nearly gave out at the first sight of him. The pallor of his skin was too familiar, and the sweatpants and T-shirt he wore were too big on him. He'd lost weight. Dread coiled my heart, constricting with lethal power. I denied the truth staring me in the face, even though Simone had laid it out straight.

"What are you doing here?" he asked, gazing past where I stood as if he expected someone else behind me.

"Simone gave me your address. Can I come in?"

"Why? You made it clear you want nothing to do with me. I'm done, Kayla."

"You can't give up."

He scowled. "She told you, didn't she?"

The air knocked from my lungs. "So it's true?"

He ushered me inside and shut the door. When we reached the living room, he sank onto the sofa and let his head fall back against the cushion.

"What kind of cancer is it?"

"A brain tumor. Inoperable."

I shook my head. "No...no. You're gonna be fine. You just need to start the chemo again. Simone said you'd stopped." Desperation clouded my tone, strained my expression.

"Kayla...no. Don't do this now. I can't handle any more pressure. I've made my peace with it."

"Well I haven't! They made a mistake. You need a second opinion."

"I got a second opinion, and a third and a fourth."

"I don't care!" I spun around, my hands clutching my hair because if I let them loose, I'd put a hole in the wall. He was going to beat this. There was no other alternative. "Gage can help. Like he helped Eve." I didn't recognize my voice, could barely see through my tears. Barely heard him through the shrill ringing in my ears.

"Our situations are completely different. Besides, we both know he won't lift a finer to help me."

"You're his brother! This goes beyond grudges." I blinked hot tears down my cheeks, hating the turbulent cyclone of terror that had taken over my stomach. "You can't die on me. You just…you can't."

"Come here." His voice held a quiet note of resignation, and I didn't like it.

Crossing the few feet between us was a no-brainer. "What do you need from me?" I whispered, drained to my soul. "What can I do?"

He opened his mouth, seemingly at a loss. "Just let me hold you."

I placed a knee onto the cushion and straddled him, squeezing his frail body with enough force to steal his breath. As I laid my head on his shoulder, he buried his face in my hair. My heart cracked in two at how much weight he'd lost.

"I dig the new haircut," he said.

"I was pissed at Gage."

His chest rumbled underneath me. "You've still got it in you."

"Instances of temporary insanity? Yeah."

He pressed his lips to my neck. "Do you remember our first kiss?"

"Of course I do."

"That kiss knocked me on my ass."

"Me too."

"That night was the most intense bout of temporary insanity ever. We were so young, so fucking clueless." He inched back and caught my gaze. "But I wouldn't change it for anything."

I leaned my forehead against his and closed my eyes, remembering the intoxicating taste of first love on my lips, the exhilarating way his fingers had slipped beneath my panties. The first time he'd pushed inside me. Like he belonged there.

Like I was home.

"I loved you so much," I said, my voice cracking.

"Past tense, Kayla?"

I only hesitated a moment. "No."

"Jesus. This isn't easy for me. I planned to go quietly."

"You would have done that to me?"

"I didn't want to put you through this." His sigh fanned across my mouth. "You chose him—"

"Ian, please..." A sob hitched in my throat. One more ding to my composure.

"Let me finish, sweetheart." He nudged the bangs from my eyes with his nose. "I don't like that you chose him, but it was your decision to make. I just...I needed to know you and Eve were okay." Tears rimmed his hazel eyes. "I can accept the cancer taking me. But leaving you...that's really killing me."

"Don't talk like that."

"I have to be realistic." He paused. "Is he still hurting you?"

I lowered my gaze.

"Tell me the truth, Kayla. No matter how ugly or hard to hear. Give it to me straight."

"He's sadistic, controlling, domineering, possessive,

jealous—"

"Sounds like a great guy," he interrupted, his mouth twisting in disdain.

"But he's also passionate…" I softened my tone. "Caring, protective. He's a disaster, but he's my disaster. And he's incredible to Eve."

"You're head over heels."

"He loves me more than I deserve."

"That's bullshit."

"It's true."

"That could never be true."

"I can't give him my whole heart."

Ian closed his eyes. "If there's anything I regret, it's not being with you in Texas. Texas could have changed everything." His chest shook with holding back what he didn't want to express in words.

I didn't think, didn't analyze the right or wrong in my actions. I only knew that he needed me. As I brought my mouth to his, I forced Gage from my mind. Shattered the images of him as I brought my fingers to the first button of my blouse.

I'd hate myself later.

Ian deserved this. *I* deserved this, because in spite of everything, Gage had taken this from us. And God, I loved that cruel and fragile man, no matter what he put me through. I forgave him for every lash, every bruise, every time he forced his will on me.

I prayed he'd find the same capacity to forgive.

"What are you doing?" Ian gazed at me with bewildered eyes.

"Giving us Texas." My fingers quaked as I unfastened a button, then another.

"Don't do this for me." He moved to push me away, but his arm was weak, ineffective in fighting me off...in fighting off his own desires. He placed his right hand on my chest, and the instant his palm conformed to the softness of my breast, he lingered until the tips of his fingers brushed my aching nipple through the thin silk of my bra.

Thrusting my breast more firmly into his hand, I let my shirt slide off my shoulders, and the garment fluttered to the floor. Desperation possessed me. Fear. The idea that the earth and everyone on it would lose him. That *I* would lose him. I pressed my mouth to his, lips parting. Tongue questing for acceptance.

He opened to me, groaning deep in his throat, and sucked my tongue into his mouth. We kissed until neither of us could breathe. I reached between us and slid my hand down the elastic band of his sweatpants, and closed my fingers around his erection.

"Jesus..." He jutted his hips, bringing him deeper into my hand. "Jesus...fuck, Kayla. Stop."

"Let me give you this."

He swallowed hard. "I want this. Jesus, I want this. But only if you're doing it for you, because I know it'll rip into your conscience."

"I don't care." I swirled my thumb through the moisture collecting at his tip. "You can't give up yet."

A hoarse groan rumbled from his throat. "This isn't going to change anything. I'm still going to have cancer

—"

"Shh. Come for me." I wanted him to purge the sickness from his body, free his mind of death and doom. "Let it out."

Live for me.

Sex was living. Loving was living. Giving in and letting go, embracing the free-fall…that was living.

Ian needed to fucking live.

I pushed to my knees, giving myself more room to work at coaxing him over the edge. As I pumped his cock with frantic strokes, illogical thoughts assaulted my sanity with trickery disguised as truth. As if I could keep him alive by making him fly.

The way Gage had made my fly while in the depths of despair over Eve's illness. My heart blanched, and another sob squeezed from my throat, except I didn't know who I was crying for now—Ian or Gage.

I was hurting both of them.

Giving one a taste of ecstasy as a bon voyage, and breaking into shards the iced-over heart of the man I'd married. The man I loved with such intensity and possessiveness and all-consuming passion that I couldn't wrap my head around what my hand was doing.

It didn't have permission, just as Ian didn't have my fucking permission to die.

Every breath he drew was a laborious, wordless plea. A plea for more. A plea for me to stop and let him go. But there was no stopping this. The orgasm came over him in a violent assault, seizing his muscles, cutting off his vocal cords. He came in a muted full-body spasm, his release spurting over my pumping fist in an unstoppable eruption. As soon as he caught his breath, my name fell from his twisted mouth, almost as if it killed him to say it.

"Why did you do that?" His eyes shuttered as he rested his head against the back of the couch.

"I…needed to."

His arms flopped like lifeless noodles at his sides. "I want to touch you. Taste you on my tongue." A tear streaked down his cheek, and there was something especially heart-wrenching about a man crying. "I'm sorry, Kayla. I never wanted to hurt you like this."

The disease had weakened him, stealing his energy reserves, the ravages of cancerous cells holding a strong man prisoner.

I folded my arms around him and sobbed, leaving tear stains on his T-shirt, and my guilt sucked the strength from me. I'd done the unforgivable. I'd betrayed Gage, and in doing so…it would change nothing. Ian would still have cancer when I walked out the door. Now that the frenzy had abated, and rational thought took hold again, I felt close to vomiting.

"I can't…" he began, his voice a mere whisper, "keep my eyes open."

"Shh, just let me hold you."

A sigh escaped him. "So tired."

"Sleep. I'm here."

"Don't want you to see me this way."

As he let sleep take him, I held on to him so tightly I thought I might never let go.

16. GOODBYE

Late afternoon shadowed Ian's living room. He was warm and breathing steadily in my arms. The clock on his end table pushed time forward, minute by minute. I was frozen, wrapped around him, holding him with everything I had.

He mumbled something in his sleep, but when I pushed back and studied him, he appeared peaceful in slumber. Healthy. Alive.

Being careful not to wake him, I slid from his lap, pushed my arms into the sleeves of my blouse and buttoned it, then went in search of a towel. I found one tucked away in a cupboard in the hallway. As I headed to the door I assumed opened into the bathroom, I pulled my cell out and dialed Simone.

She answered before the first ring completed. "Did you talk to him?"

"Yeah." Swallowing hard, I blinked back tears. "He's made up his mind."

"You gotta keep trying."

"I will," I said as I entered the bathroom. "But I need you to do something for me." I held the phone between my shoulder and ear as I turned on the faucet in the bathroom and dampened a blue cotton towel.

"What do you need?"

"Can you pick up Eve from school and keep her for the night?"

"Sure thing. I'll get someone to cover the last couple hours of my shift."

"Thank you." I squeezed the excess water from the towel before exiting the bathroom. "You're already on the list for picking her up." Pausing halfway to the living room, I lowered my voice. "If Gage calls you, tell him you haven't heard from me."

"What's going on?" The alarm in her tone unnerved me. She had reason to be concerned. *I* had reason to be terrified because there was no way of knowing how he'd react when I returned home.

"Nothing to worry about," I told her. What a blatant lie. "We're going to need some time to talk, and it's best if Eve isn't around for that."

"Kayla," she warned.

"It's okay. I can handle it."

"Call me *immediately* if you need me."

"I will." I halted at the entrance to the living room, where Ian lay sprawled on the couch where I'd left him. His sweatpants were a mess from his cum, and I realized I probably had it on my skirt as well.

I told Simone I'd talk to her later before hanging up and making my way into Ian's bedroom to hunt for a clean pair of pants. When I returned to him, he was mumbling in his sleep again. I placed the clothing onto the cushion next to him and worked the soiled sweats down his thighs.

His lashes fluttered open. "Hey, beautiful."

"Hey." Bringing the towel to his lap, I cleaned him up as quickly as I could, trying to avoid embarrassing him.

"You don't have to do that. I'm not an invalid."

I glanced into his stormy eyes. "I know you're not. I just want to help. Let me help." I had to do something, even if it was something as simple as cleaning up the mess we'd made and helping him into a fucking pair of clean pants.

He let me do so grudgingly, and then he patted his lap.

I wanted so badly to go to him, but if I put myself in that position again, I wasn't sure I'd be able to stop at touching him.

"It's okay. I understand," he said, reading the indecision spreading across my face. He leaned forward and rubbed his head.

"Is it a headache?"

"Yeah." He rose to his feet, taking a few seconds to gain solid footing. As he moved toward the kitchen, his left arm hanging limply at his side, I realized he was having trouble using it.

My lips trembled. Grief stung my eyes and nose. But I refused to give in to my weakness. He needed me to be strong right now, and I needed him to keep fighting.

I followed him into the kitchen. "I need you to do

something for me."

"Anything."

"Go back on the chemo."

He frowned. "Anything but that."

"Please, Ian. Don't give up."

"I fought for six months." He grabbed a pill box and single-handedly flipped the lid on one of the sections. "I don't have anything left."

"You have *me*," I said, my voice and soul splintering in two.

He dropped the pills into his mouth and washed them down with a swig of water. "We both know that's not true."

Unable to argue with him, I found myself speechless.

He set the glass of water on the counter with a loud thud before spanning the few feet between us.

"Ian," I said, my heart pounding something fierce as he backed me against the refrigerator. The stainless steel chilled me to my bones.

He fingered a strand of my hair before lowering his right hand to my collared neck. "Does he make you happy?"

"Most of the time." My guilt leaked through the fissure in my soul. I tried ignoring the lingering scent of Ian's cum on my body, but I couldn't, just as I couldn't ignore what I'd done.

"Don't tell him about this, Kayla. He doesn't need to know."

I nodded, even though I knew I would tell Gage. Not only tell him, but beg for forgiveness. Keeping this bottled inside would end me. And Gage would know anyway. He'd spot the treachery in my eyes as soon as he walked into the house.

"Thank you for loving me too," he said.

I clung to his T-shirt, burying my face in the soft fabric, and cried. "You're saying goodbye."

"Yes."

"Why are you giving up?"

"I refuse to spend the last few weeks I have left on chemo."

"But it could save your life!" I fisted my hands and pounded against his chest, hoping to beat some sense into him. "Please, Ian. *Please*. It could work. Look at Eve! She —"

"It's different!" He halted my furious fists with his working arm. "My fucking brain is quitting on me. I can't do this anymore. The chemo wasn't working. The tumor isn't going away. It's only getting worse." His chest stilled as if he were holding his breath. "I'd rather go with dignity. On *my* terms. You need to accept that."

"Why do you have to be so damn stubborn?"

"It's in my blood."

That was true. Gage shared that same blood. But could he find it in his heart to forgive Ian before it was too late? I honestly didn't know, especially after what we'd done on the couch less than two hours ago. I never believed myself capable of betraying Gage, but I had. I'd done the unthinkable. The unforgivable.

And I couldn't find the strength to regret it, other than for the pain it would cause him. I gulped just thinking of how he'd react—how I was about to tear his heart out.

"You should go home."

"Who's going to take care of you?"

"I'll be okay. Stop worrying about me."

"That's impossible."

"This is why I didn't want you to know."

"Then why did you meet me in that coffee shop?"

"*Not* seeing you was impossible. I've thought of nothing else since I walked out of your hospital room a year ago."

"But why now?" I already knew, heard the words before he spoke them.

"In some irrational part of my brain, I thought if I could win you back, maybe I'd have more reason to fight." He frowned. "But I realized it wasn't fair to you. It's not your job to give me a fucking reason to live."

"If you need a reason, I'll give you one."

He lifted a brow. "Are you willing to divorce him?"

I gaped at him, unable to find words because I didn't like the answer. Even now, faced with his illness, I'd still choose Gage.

"I knew the answer before I asked, Kayla. And I'd never ask that of you anyway. I'm just making a point. You can't give me a reason. I have to *want* to fight, and I did fight. I tried all kinds of treatments. But some things can't be fixed."

"Don't say that."

"It is what it is!" He stepped back, no longer touching me. "You need to accept it."

"Please. I'm begging you."

"And I'm begging you to go home. I can't argue with you about this anymore."

I leaned against the refrigerator, frozen in that position for what seemed like forever with my hands balled at my sides.

"Jesus, Kayla. You told me in my office that being near me was torture. Well this is worse. I need you to go. Please, just go."

"Okay," I choked out. As I left his house with tears dripping down my cheeks, splattering the ground with despair, the ache in my gut shoved the truth into my head. Into my heart.

This was goodbye.

17. MISTAKE

Gage found me naked and kneeling in the basement, the bullwhip coiled in front of me, waiting to strike me like a snake. The thing *ticked, ticked, ticked* like a rattler in my mind. Or maybe that was time ticking by, bringing me a second closer to the annihilation of my marriage.

To the sharp sting of leather that, for the first time, I'd gladly welcome. I wanted the strikes to take away my pain—pound to dust Ian's illness and my shame over what I'd done.

He halted in front of me, his shiny black shoes coming into view. I tilted my head and wanted to sink through the floor as his suspicious gaze flickered between the bullwhip and my face.

"Where's Eve?" he asked.

"Gone for the night."

He knelt before me and held my chin between two harsh fingers. "I called you hours ago. Where were you?"

No words or explanation could express the chaos inside me. I thought I was void of tears, but I was wrong.

I'd been so, so wrong for betraying him like this.

"I'm sorry," I said, a sob squeezing from my throat. This was going to hurt him so much, and the knowledge rose like acid.

"Baby…" He broke me to pieces by brushing the tears from my cheeks. Doubt colored his features, and in that moment, I read him so easily, had an idea of what he was thinking.

Maybe he was wrong. Maybe the dread in his gut was lying to him.

"What's wrong? Is Eve okay?"

"S-she's fine." I swallowed hard. "I did something you're going to hate me for." I lifted the whip and pressed it against his thighs. "I didn't mean to hurt you. I… God…" Shaking my head, I let the tears drop.

"Just tell me." A familiar tick went off in his jaw.

"I saw Ian."

"What do you mean you saw him?" He furrowed his brows. "Because I know my wife, the woman I love more than anything in this world, would never *see* my brother."

"More than saw him," I said, my voice a croak that echoed my shame. He pushed away, and the whip crashed to the floor.

I grasped it by the handle, scrambled to my feet, and offered him the implement I feared the most. The one I deserved the most.

"Please, Gage—" Everything inside me fractured. "Strike me with it. I deserve nothing less." I couldn't bear the devastation my words drilled into his eyes. Every emotion he rotated through came off him in a tangible blast.

I hadn't voiced my sin, but he heard it anyway. He stumbled back, hands clenched at his sides, shaking with the need to punish. To maim the way I'd maimed him.

"Gage, please."

"What did you do?" he asked between tight lips.

"I…" I'd never felt so broken, so helpless. He'd taken me to hell and back, but it turned out my actions were the final accomplice in my destruction. "It just…happened."

"You fucked him." No question, only harsh certainty.

"No." The denial felt like a lie. "Let me explain."

"God, Kayla—" His voice broke, and that anguished sound alone brought tears to my eyes. He buried both hands in his hair and paced the room like a lost man. "I don't want to hear it. The reasons don't fucking matter."

"Please—"

"Nothing you say will justify you cheating on me with *him*!" He propped his back against the wall and slid to his haunches.

I couldn't fix this. I'd done the unforgivable, and I absolutely could *not* fix this. After everything we'd been through, I'd hit him in the one place capable of destroying him.

"I'll do anything," I said, forcing the words out beyond my constricted throat. "It was a mistake."

"A *mistake*? We're fucking married. This isn't like Texas when you had a choice to make."

"You didn't give me a choice!" Probably the wrong time to point that out, but I couldn't help it.

"I gave you a choice!" his voice bellowed through the

basement, making my muscles lock and tense. My legs threatened to go out on me. He jumped to his feet and stormed to where I stood with the bullwhip gripped in my nervous hands.

"On your fucking knees. *Now*."

And just like that, I dropped. Groveled at his feet. Let my tears bathe the floor.

"I gave you a choice," he repeated, calmer this time. "I dragged your stubborn ass back home, but right here in this spot, I gave you the option to walk."

"I couldn't."

"Why?"

"You know why."

He let out a cruel, bitter laugh. "You claim you love me but—"

"I do love you."

"Then why? Make me understand how you could *almost* fuck my brother after I gave you what you wanted on our anniversary? I gave you everything, Kayla. *Everything!*"

My mouth trembled as the truth stalled, frozen on my tongue. I didn't want to say it, but not voicing Ian's illness wouldn't make it go away. "He has a brain tumor."

He blinked. "A…what?" That hadn't been the answer he was expecting.

"When I found out…" I hiccuped, holding back another sob. "I was blindsided. Simone called me, otherwise, I wouldn't have known. I wouldn't have gone to see him."

He shook his head, disbelieving, and I rushed to

explain.

"He's refusing treatment." My limbs quaked in defeat, and only my willpower to obey him kept me on my knees instead of sprawled on the floor. "He's got a few weeks left."

His jaw worked in a frightful way, and his eyes brightened with the threat of tears. No matter the decrepit bridge between him and his brother, this news affected him.

But my betrayal was the real clincher. I slumped, and as I dragged the memory of what I'd done to the forefront of my mind, my ashamed gaze fell to the floor. I didn't understand how I'd ended up on that couch with Ian, my hand in his pants, my lips pressed to his.

"Get into position and look at me." His tone left no room for argument.

Letting the bullwhip slip from my grasp, I forced my body to fucking work. I dredged the last of my strength and straightened my spine. Hands behind my back, breasts thrust out. Eyes on him.

"How far did it go?" he asked...no, *demanded*.

"Please don't make me tell you." My cheeks flamed under his scrutiny.

"How far, Kayla?"

"We kissed."

"What else? You're going to tell me every detail."

He was going to make me drown in my guilt. "I took my shirt off, and I...I..."

"You *what*?"

"I touched him. I made him—" The word hitched in

my throat. I couldn't do it. I couldn't describe Ian coming. And no matter how long I analyzed my behavior, I couldn't explain what had been going through my mind while I'd had my cheating hand around his brother's cock.

"Spell it out for me, and address me properly when you do."

"I jerked him off, Master."

"Look at me."

I lifted my gaze, realizing after the fact that I'd been staring at his shoes. "I'm sorry, Master."

"Do not lower your eyes again." He took a step closer. "Did his cock fill your hand the way mine does? Did you want to take him in your mouth?"

His caustic tone made me nauseous—so fucking sick to my stomach that I couldn't speak.

"Answer me!"

"I don't know! I don't know what I was thinking." I held my chest, as if to keep my heart from spilling to the ground. "Whip me, Master. I'm begging you."

He kicked the bullwhip out of reach. "I'm not taking this away for you. You did it, now you get to deal with the consequences."

I bent at the waist, nearly falling sideways. I'd never regretted something so much in my life. If I could take it back...

But would I? Knowing that I might never see Ian again? Never touch him or hear his voice?

He was *dying*. But the reasons didn't matter to Gage. There were no ands, ifs, or buts with him. Only obedience and my unconditional loyalty.

"Please, Gage. I need you so much right now." I was a selfish bitch for needing him to comfort me in my time of grief when I'd broken his heart.

"Don't move," he said through clenched teeth. "When I get back, your knees better be redder than your damn cheeks."

"Where are you going?" I crawled after him, reaching with desperate fingers, hysteria rising and careening through me, pushing me to the edge of deranged.

"I said don't move!" His contempt rained down on me as I kneeled at his feet.

"Yes, Master," I choked out, closing my eyes and letting my tears burn my face.

I listened to his unsteady breathing, his fight to hold it together. "I love you so damn much, Kayla." A pause...a beat of irreparable damage passing us by. "But right now I need to clear my fucking head."

My eyes flew open, and through my misery, I watched him climb the stairs. His feet raged war with each stomp. He wrenched the door open, and an instant later the light went out. A ricocheting bang signaled his exit. My stomach heaved and erupted, and I spewed my fear all over the floor.

The interesting thing about darkness was how it amplified everything—silence, the pungent smell of puke, even the unfaithful heart beating a furious tempo behind my breastbone. I pushed to my knees and clasped my hands at my back.

And I waited.

18. HOW TO SAVE A LIFE

Gage returned some time later. The light switched on before his heavy feet brought him down the stairs. He stopped in front of me, where I'd kneeled like a statue for the past...three hours, maybe? The only thing I knew for certain was how badly my knees ached. How my whole body ached.

"Can I please stand, Master?"

He grasped me by the shoulders and helped me hobble to the bed. My legs were numb, full of tingles, and I could hardly walk without his support. I sat at the end and waited for him to speak. The way the corners of his mouth twitched told me he had much to say.

He sat next to me and entwined his hands as if to keep them busy, so he didn't lose control and use them on me. "I went to see Ian," he said.

I held my breath, my heart pounding too loudly in my ears.

He lowered his head. "He's my fucking brother, Kayla, but all I could think about as I looked at him was you." Pushing to his feet, he paced the area in front of me. "You touching him, kissing him, fucking jerking him off."

"Gage, I'm sorr—"

"Let me finish." He pushed a hand through his hair in agitation. "I'm rotten to the soul because all I could think about was how his death would affect you. Call me a selfish bastard, but I don't want you grieving him. He doesn't deserve it."

I held my breath, deliberating between anticipation and dread.

"So I convinced him to check into a special treatment center out of state." He held up a hand, silencing anything I might say. "I love you enough to give you the world, and that includes doing everything in my power to save his life."

To say I was shocked was an understatement. "Master —"

"Can you *shut up* and listen?"

I nodded, clamping my lips.

"But that doesn't mean my motives are selfless. He's leaving in two days, and you won't ever see him again." He paused, and the hard line of his mouth put me on alert. "It doesn't matter if he lives or dies, Kayla because he agreed not to come back. I made it clear that if he comes near Oregon, or contacts you in any way, I will punish you for it."

Gage knew how to play people to perfection. Ian loved me enough to stay away. I hoped to God he loved me enough to live.

"I own you." Gage bent and twisted his fingers in my hair, jerking my head back. "With the exception of Eve, there is no one else in your world but me. Do you understand?"

"Yes, Master," I said, my words drifting across his lips in a breathless whisper.

"You had better, because I'm demanding every last molecule of your heart."

"I understand, Master. I never meant for any of this to happen. If I could take it back, I would."

"Well, when you fuck around with temptation, you get burned." He let me go, rose to his full height, and crossed his arms.

"I hate myself for ruining your trust in me."

"You think I forbade you to see him because I didn't trust you? Fuck, trust has nothing to do with it. It's just cold, harsh reality. You're weak when it comes to your greedy cunt, and even weaker when it comes to your heart. I exploited that, baby." He paused long enough to let out a cruel laugh. "I can't even blame you for it because I *knew* you loved him. Hell, Kayla, I wrecked any fucking chance you had with him from the moment I forced your legs apart."

Matching action to words, he bent and slipped a hand between my thighs. "Spread them, now."

"Yes, Master." I opened wide for him, and he feathered his fingers so lightly over my pussy that I wasn't sure if he meant to touch me at all.

"I stole you from him," he said, voice ragged. "And I'd do it again. I have no remorse or shame in making you mine. My only regret is allowing you to stumble."

"I did that on my own."

"No, you didn't. I own you, which means I own your mistakes. And you can be sure this one won't happen again. That taste of freedom you got? Savor it. This is the last time I leave you to your own devices."

Unable to speak, I simply nodded. My heart beat in a frenzied tune of fear. I'd backtracked us by months… years possibly.

"I confiscated your cell and the key to your car. It'll be a frozen day in hell before you get them back." He gave my inner thigh a sound slap. "Thank me for disciplining you."

"Thank you, Master."

His fingers pinched my thigh. "Beg me to punish you."

"Punish me, Master. Please." I gazed at him through my tears, meaning every word, despite the terror of the unknown rising in the form of vomit. "I deserve whatever you decide."

He palmed my cheek. "This decision wasn't easy for me. I want you to know that. But I feel this is the only way to ensure you never stumble again."

I swallowed hard, barely getting past the huge lump of terror in my throat. "What are you planning to do to me?"

He dipped a finger between my legs, crooking it in just the right way. "No orgasms for the duration of your punishment. That's a start." He stood and gestured to the bed on which I sat. "You'll sleep here tonight."

I blinked a tear down my cheek. God, this hurt. The distance growing between us, the way he couldn't quite look me in the eye. I already missed him.

But he'd gotten Ian help. If anything good came from this, it was the chance Ian now had at living.

19. PROPERTY OF GAGE CHANNING

He made me sleep in the basement for a week. I did my best to act normally when Eve was home, which was the only time he let me out, but it was harder than I thought. I missed my daughter. I missed my freedom.

I missed him.

One mistake had destroyed our happiness, and I wasn't sure how long it would take to get that back. But I had to try. No matter what he had in store for me, I had to do everything in my power to earn his forgiveness.

On the eighth morning, the door creaked open, just like it had during the previous week. Like clockwork, he brought my meals down to the basement. As he descended the stairs, I wiped my cheeks, certain I had tear stains on them from crying so much.

Every night as I fell asleep, first thing in the morning, and every time he left me alone in his dungeon. The separation was killing me. I wished he would punish me and get it over with, even if it meant taking strikes from every implement of pain he owned.

His heavy feet landed on the bottom step, and I realized something was different about today. He wasn't dressed for work, and he wasn't carrying a plate of food.

"Strip," he ordered.

I peeled the long T-shirt I'd been sleeping in from my body.

"Put on a pair of heels." He gestured toward the collection of stilettos against the wall, right under his paddles and floggers.

I crossed the room, selected a red pair because I knew he liked the color, then slid my feet into them, one by one. As I bent over, I missed the way my hair used to curtain my face, trailing toward the ground. Straightening my spine, I faced him. And I waited.

He held out a hand.

"Come here."

I went to the hand beckoning me, as eager as a well-trained dog. Knowing this didn't change a thing. I gladly slipped my palm into his.

"Today you begin the first day of your punishment."

Something ominous tingled down my spine. We climbed the stairs in silence—the kind of quiet that was the polar opposite of comfortable. As he led me through the house, I wanted to ask questions.

What are you going to do to me?

Will it hurt?

Will you ever forgive me?

He pulled a keyring from his pocket and unlocked his office. This was a new development, as he'd never felt the need to lock his office before now, and that made me question what waited on the other side of that door.

Fitting his hand to the small of my back, he ushered me inside, and that's when I spied the cage standing upright in a corner, barely big enough to fit one person.

I gulped.

"For every day that Ian is in treatment, you will spend your time in that cage while Eve is in school. I've arranged to work from home for a few weeks."

Paying attention to the intricate details, I inspected the cage and guessed he planned to put me in there facing the corner. There was an open area about the right height for my ass.

I cast a pleading glance his way. "Please don't do this, Master."

"I didn't do this. You did."

"I don't blame you for being angry."

"Kayla, I'm not angry. I'm fucking destroyed."

"I'm sorry," I said, falling to my knees and kissing his bare feet. I was that desperate.

"I know you are, and that's why I know you'll take your sentence with gratitude. I expect you to thank me every goddam day for it." He grasped my hair with his unyielding fingers. "Get up."

I was certain my heart was about to claw its way out of my chest and die a slow, torturous death on the floor. I hadn't been this scared in a long time. That cage seemed larger than life with its door wide open and waiting for me to cross the threshold.

I cast a nervous glance at Gage. "I'll do anything else. Anything."

"Begging won't save you from this."

My voice rose to an unnatural level. "Please—"

"What I did for *him*," he interrupted, "I did for you." He gestured to the small prison. "Now you're going to do this for me."

He was punishing me for wanting Ian to live, and in a way, he was also punishing his brother. The longer Ian fought the cancer, the longer Gage would imprison me. He was possibly the most sadistic man on the planet.

"When it's over, will you forgive me, Master?"

For the first time in days, he touched me. Raising his palms, he framed my cheeks. "Pay your penance, baby, then we'll talk forgiveness." He swept away my tears with his thumbs, and it was those sparks of gentleness, of compassion, that kept me forever under his spell.

But with that spark of empathy also burned an ember of a wound that wouldn't heal anytime soon. My week spent in the basement hadn't softened him a bit. I deserved the consequences, but knowing what I was in for and getting it were two different things. I eyed the cage with its cold bars, various hooks and stockades, and shivered.

"Don't move." He crossed to his desk and pulled a ball gag out of a drawer, along with a set of nipple clamps and leather cuffs. I stood like an inanimate object —save for the shivers of my naked body—as he revealed the biggest, most gag-worthy contraption of rubber he owned.

"Gage—"

"I'm your Master right now. Not your lover, not your

husband. I'm your fucking Master, and you *will* obey me."
He held the rubber ball in front of my trembling lips.
"Open your mouth."

"Can we talk about this?" I asked in a rush. "I know
what I did hurt—"

"Kayla, open your mouth now."

Seconds passed—silent, agonizing seconds that
weighed heavily on us. I realized that nothing I said would
help my case or absolve me of my sin. My temporary
moment of insanity didn't matter because, on the most
fundamental level, I'd betrayed him.

My terror of enduring that cage didn't matter. He
would impose his will on me until I relented, and he'd do
it because that's what he needed to get past what I'd done.

I swallowed hard, utter dread coiling around my neck
like a boa constrictor. The collar I wore, the ring on my
finger—both bound me to the spot with the inescapable
strength of chains. Parting my lips, I let him inch the ball
in, allowing the contraption to spread my mouth
unbearably wide…wider still until the gag filled every
crevice. He fastened the strap around my head, and I
drew in slow breaths through my nose to calm my raging
pulse.

To quiet the panic that flared inside me.

Saliva collected on my tongue and threatened to leak
past my lips. The gag would have me drooling like a fool
in no time. That was the thing I hated most about being
gagged. The humiliation and the accompanying saliva that
would drip down my chin before landing on my breasts.

"Give me your hands."

I met his eyes and pleaded for mercy. Mostly, I hated not having a voice, despised not being heard. Another tear fell as he buckled leather cuffs around my wrists.

"You lied to me when you promised to stay away from him," he said, moving on to my ankles. "Which is why you're going to endure that gag." He stood and gripped my chin. "Blink if you understand."

I blinked, and blinked some more. One, two, three times with deliberate meaning.

Forgive me, Master.

"Stop it." He took my nipples between two fingers and pinched. "Did he touch your nipples?" He tilted his head and studied me, almost as if my forced silence would answer. "He did, didn't he?" He gave them a hard twist. "Did he make them hurt like this? Or maybe he sucked on them. I know how much you like your nipples played with." He let go and lowered a hand between my legs. "Did he touch you here? Did he fuck you with his fingers? Maybe he even dipped his tongue into *my* cunt. Did you let him taste what's mine, Kayla?"

My body reacted to his touch, to the images they produced in my poisoned head, and I spread my legs a little wider.

"Did you spread your legs for him?" He thrust angry, punishing fingers inside me, bringing me to my toes, wrenching a pleading moan from my gagged mouth.

Sick. I was so sick. He was about to discipline me for the ultimate sin, and I couldn't stop from dripping onto his fingers, down his wrist.

Who knew self-loathing could be so toxic?

"I'm going to take your flushed cheeks as a yes." He stepped closer until we were nose to nose. "But *I'm* the one who owns you. I'm the one who decides when you come. The only one who decides if you ever come again." His claim to my pussy took on the tempo of a jackhammer, fingers plundering my slick heat. "I'm the one who decides if you ever talk again. If you ever exist outside of that cage again."

I wanted so badly to be strong, but my moans gurgled in my throat, barely held back, and my eyes begged him for more. I pushed my breasts out, hoping the tightness of my nipples would distract him. Tempt him.

But Gage was a man of his word. Stubborn, steadfast, and immovable. No amount of temptation would appeal to him because he was in his *zone*—that dangerous place where the only thing that tempted him was my pain and humiliation.

"We *will* get past this." He positioned himself in front of me, feet shoulder-width apart on the floor, his fist clenching a set of nipple clamps. "Because I love you."

I felt my eyes widen at the change in his tone. The hope it brought forth.

"I'll find a way to forgive you for this, because you've forgiven me for so much shit, Kayla." He clamped my nipples, and then I stood before him, his decorated slave. He gestured to the awaiting prison. "Inside, now."

Oh God.

That space seemed so tight. On shaking limbs, I obeyed and tried not to squirm as I faced the corner, but it was futile. Gooseflesh licked my ass, a precursor to what I instinctively knew. He was going to whip me through the opening of the cage. Maybe not now. Maybe not even today.

But eventually, he would take the bullwhip to my ass.

"Good girl." He spread my arms out, locking my wrists to the bars at my sides. Then he used a foot to nudge my feet apart so he could anchor them as well. After he finished securing me, I stood in four-inch heels, spread-eagled, and incapable of moving or even shifting my weight.

Panic took hold of me, increasing my heart rate, making me breathe heavily through my nose. How would I stand this, day in and day out?

I honestly didn't know.

20. SENTENCE

I cracked after three days of imprisonment. Locked inside his cage of hell with my mouth gagged and nipples clamped, my wrists and ankles bound—I cried harder than I'd ever cried before. Sobs wrenched from my gut, and I worried I was close to hyperventilating.

Snot ran from my nose, mixing with the saliva escaping the gag. I was a hot mess. A blubbering mess. A mess he mostly ignored, other than to free me for ten minutes every two hours so I could move around and regain circulation. So I could eat and use the bathroom.

So I could feel like a fucking human being again for the small amount of time he allowed.

He had yet to strike me with anything, but just being inside this contraption was soul-sucking, and thinking of the endless weeks to come…

I was going insane, my mind shattering, my nerves teetering on the ledge. If Gage intended to make me forget about Ian, he'd done a bang up job because his idea of imprisonment tormented me to the point that I couldn't think of *anything* else.

The touch of his warm hands on my ass cheeks startled me. My chest heaved every couple of seconds, spasming with sobs.

"Baby, calm down. Getting so worked up isn't going to help."

Calm down? *Calm down?* My mind screamed at him because I sure as fuck couldn't do it vocally.

He slid his finger between my legs, and that had an immediate effect. Not necessarily a calming one, but it was something.

"I'm trying to work, but you're over here about to have a panic attack." He plunged a finger into my pussy. Instantly, arousal flared. It had been over two weeks since he'd let me come. But even worse, two weeks had gone by since I'd slept at his side.

"If you can calm down and behave, I'll think about making you come tonight."

I shook my head, protesting despite the gag. I only wanted him—like a druggie craving the next fix. Like a child craving candy. Like I craved Gage Channing.

"So you *don't* want to come?" He sounded surprised and amused. He smacked my ass hard. "You want me to punish you?"

I shook my head again.

Another smack brought me to my toes. The impact of his palm tingled over my skin, more arousing than painful. I heard him insert a key, and the door squeaked open. He unbuckled the gag then wiped my face with a napkin.

"What does my naughty prisoner want then?"

"Master, I want to sleep in our bed tonight."

"Why do you want that?"

Another sob hitched. "I miss you so much. Please, Master. I will stand here all day without making a sound if you'll just hold me tonight."

I heard him suck in a breath, which gave me hope because he didn't seem as collected as he would have me believe.

"Behave yourself, and we'll see."

He reinserted the gag, and for the next few hours, I stood silent and still, determined more than ever to do as I was told. When afternoon rolled around, and he freed me so I could tend to Eve, I'd allowed hope to settle in, and hope was a dangerous thing when it came to a man like Gage, especially considering how angry and hurt he was over my actions. Today he'd been gentle, even kind, but on other days, he'd had nothing but snide remarks and scornful planes on his gorgeous face.

My mistake had snowballed into something horrific and ugly, and I worried no time in the world could erase what I'd done, could patch his heart back together. Or mine, for that matter.

"What's wrong, Mommy?"

I picked at my salad that night at dinner. "Nothing baby. I'm just tired." I mustered a smile and met her inquisitive gaze. "How was school?"

"At lunch, I sat with Vanessa and Toby."

"What happened to Leah?"

Eve's face crumbled. "She said she's not my friend

anymore."

Her sadness pricked at my heart. "Why did she say that?"

Rather than answer, Eve shrugged and spooned in a bite of mashed potatoes.

"Answer your mother, Eve."

She sat up straight upon hearing his no-bullshit tone. It was a tone I knew well, and though I appreciated him backing me up, it also bothered me that he often talked to us both in the same manner.

Like children, only Eve *was* my child.

"She said I was being mean, but I wasn't."

"Did she tell you why she thought that?"

Her lower lip poked out. "Some kids called her names. She said I wasn't her friend anymore because I laughed."

"Did you say you're sorry? That wasn't very nice."

"I wasn't laughing at her, Mommy! The names were funny."

"Princess, just tell her you're sorry, and you didn't mean it." Gage's attention landed on me. "People make mistakes. I'm sure she'll forgive you."

I held my breath for a full minute, unable to erase his words from my mind. I wanted to believe that forgiveness was possible, that we could find our way back to each other, but the road ahead seemed endless and full of rocky mountains I'd have to climb over first.

I came across the first rocky hill later that night after Eve went to bed. I'd been so out of my mind all week with being locked in that cage, that I failed to realize tonight was Friday.

Gage had no problem reminding me. A little after 11 p.m., I found myself bent over the end of our bed, my fingers gripping my skirt and exposing my ass to him. Only this time he wasn't using his belt.

He gripped the bullwhip.

"Master, I'm scared."

"You should be."

"Please don't hurt me."

"Did you stop to think how your cheating would hurt me?"

"Yes, Master."

"But you touched him anyway." The tail cracked an instant before the strike landed. My entire body tensed. I remained silent, but only because the pain knocked the air from my lungs. Before I was able to catch my breath, he struck again.

I tried managing my breathing, willed my muscles to relax and accept the brutality of his arm, but my screams fractured the air. After the twentieth lash, he dropped the whip, pulled the drawer to our nightstand open, and grabbed a tube of cream.

A groan almost escaped me as he applied the ointment to the reddening welts on my backside. I knew I wouldn't be able to sit for a while.

"Do you still want to sleep in our bed?"

My heart skipped. "Yes, Master."

He crossed the room and turned off the light. I didn't move from my bent over position at the end of the mattress. He scooped me into his arms, stunning me into a boneless mess, and tucked me against him under the sheets. His warm embrace surrounded me, and my heart wouldn't stop thumping a furious beat as I sank into him.

The intensity of the moment washed over me, and I drew on the vestiges of my strength to hold back my tears.

"I know I've been harsh with you."

I didn't know how to answer that. His punishment was more than I could bear, yet I understood him. No sane person would, but he was my crazy, and I understood him. I also knew how deep his hurt ran. His wounds would bleed for a long time, slow to scab over.

"I'm sorry I hurt you, Master."

"I know, baby." He nuzzled my neck. "Get some sleep."

For the first time in two weeks, I slept in complete harmony, wrapped in my husband's arms.

21. THE OTHER WOMAN

Eve didn't have school on Monday, so I got a break from the cage. While Gage worked in his office, I spent most of the day playing with her. We battled each other in the game of Life, made up our own rules for Monopoly, and played Go Fish for hours.

It was freeing to have so much time to myself. A whole day with my daughter. A whole day of not having to set foot inside that cage. Things were looking up. Gage hadn't sent me to the basement since he'd allowed me back into our bed, and he'd held me every single night, though he still refused to make love to me.

He wouldn't even fuck me, nor did he use my mouth for his pleasure. I'd heard him groaning his release in the shower over the weekend, more than once, finding satisfaction by his own hand. I wasn't worthy enough for him to fuck, and that stung. The spooning at night, however…that I couldn't complain about. It was all he could offer me now, and I'd eat it up like a starved animal.

But Tuesdays came around like they always did. I'd

never despised a Tuesday with such intensity, but with Eve back in school, Gage didn't hesitate in returning me to the cage. As he held the gag in front of my lips, I thanked him for his discipline and accepted the rubber ball. I behaved like a model prisoner for fear that he'd send me back to the basement if I lost my shit again.

The days came and went, most of them spent within the confines of those bars. My bars of shame. My bars of penance. In the back of my mind, I knew to be grateful for each day in that contraption because it meant Ian was still fighting. The day when the cage became no more…I couldn't allow my thoughts to go there.

But two months, three weeks, and five days later, that day crashed through my world like a wrecking ball.

"Why are you taking me down here?" I asked as Gage ushered me through the door of the basement.

"Your time in the cage is over."

I froze on the bottom step, my heart in my throat. Looking over my shoulder, I opened my mouth to ask the one thing he wouldn't want to hear.

"Don't even think about it, Kayla. It doesn't matter if he lived or died. All you need to know is that you're free of your prison now."

"Master, I'm beggin—"

"I suggest you don't, unless you'd like an additional two months in that prison."

I clamped my mouth shut, shaking my head, but in the back of my mind, resolve formed. Some way, some how, I'd learn of Ian's fate.

"Let's get on with this," Gage said, pulling me back to

the current moment.

"Get on with what?"

"The last phase of your punishment." He grabbed my arm and led me into the middle of the basement. I expected him to order me to strip. Instead, he pulled me into his arms. "We need to be able to trust each other. That's going to take some time."

"I know," I whispered, my face hidden in the fabric of his shirt. I squeezed my eyes shut, willing away the burn in them.

"I'm going to make love to you for hours."

I held onto him with more strength, unashamed of the moan that rumbled from my throat. His words hit me right between the thighs. His erection grew, pressing against my stomach, and his chest rose and fell too quickly.

"It's been too fucking long, baby. Punishing you was torture."

"I've missed you so much."

"Me too," he said, nuzzling the crown of my head. He held on for a few seconds longer before letting go. "Strip."

Anxiety stormed through my veins as I removed the T-shirt and sleep shorts I'd worn that morning while seeing Eve off to school. As I stood motionless, my skin erupting in goose bumps while my nipples puckered, he sorted through his toys.

"Get into position at the cross," he said, his back to me.

The air in the basement seemed chillier than usual. Or

maybe the tremor in my limbs stemmed from fear because I had no idea what he had in store for me.

The last phase of my punishment…that could mean anything.

I moved the few feet to the St. Andrew's cross and aligned my body with it. He joined me, holding the cuffs that would hold me at his mercy, along with the gag that would silence my ability to beg for any.

But I was eager to end this torturous sentence. Frantic to have my husband back. My grief over Ian's illness had caused me to stumble, but Gage had scraped it out with his psychological confines. Now I brimmed with his will.

A small piece of my heart still hurt when I thought of Ian, but my husband, my Master had crashed through any remaining barriers by locking me inside that cage. He'd conditioned me back to a state of total obedience. I didn't put up a smidgen of fight when he anchored me to the cross. Didn't protest when he pushed the gag into my mouth.

He stepped back and perused his possession, and as his gaze wandered over my exposed and vulnerable body, something dark flashed in his eyes.

I didn't like that look. That indigo glint was an omen of bad things to come.

He reached into his pocket and drew out his cell, brought it to his ear with calculation. "You can come down now."

Silence screamed between us as the minutes ticked by. He said nothing, and I *couldn't* say anything. Then the door at the top of the stairs creaked open, and time seemed to screech to a violent halt as Katherine descended, tainting *our* space with her rancid presence.

Reality was a fragile thing, too easily shattered by the figments of our imaginations. Because what I was seeing couldn't be real. No way was Katherine standing beside Gage while I was naked and chained to the cross.

The old Gage would have done something this wicked—this fucked-up and *wrong*—but not the Gage I'd married. His brutal side had owned my punishment, but we'd moved past Katherine.

Hadn't we?

So why the hell was she standing there, her mouth curled in a triumphant smirk?

Memories of the last time the three of us had occupied this room blew through my head like a category five hurricane. Ian and Katherine on the couch. Gage forcing me over the bed and fucking me hard so he could torture his brother. So he could exact revenge.

Was this his grand finale of revenge on me? Was he going to make me watch him fuck Katherine, bent over the bed, slamming into her with the force of his anger? I almost retched at the thought, and only the knowledge that I'd choke on my vomit held it at bay.

The severity of his mouth scared the hell out of me. I could tolerate him fucking me in front of her, using my body for his sadistic pleasure. I could even tolerate him subjecting me to degradation.

I could *not* handle watching him touch that bitch.

God, had he experienced this same all-consuming jealousy at the thought of me with Ian? Roiling and ravishing the spirit like a monstrous storm? No wonder he'd locked me in a cage.

He pulled his shirt over his head, and my thought processes crashed into a cement wall. His shirt lay discarded on the floor at his feet.

Pound, pound, pound.

My heart became its own entity behind my ribcage, taking on a rhythm of unnatural origin. No one's heart should beat this hard and fast—not without sending them into cardiac arrest.

He turned to Katherine. "On your knees," he said, setting his hands on her shoulders and applying pressure until she kneeled before him.

"Unbutton my pants."

Undiluted rage coursed through me. I lurched forward, wrenching my wrists as far as the restraints allowed. She brought her fingers to his pants and followed his command.

"Unzip me."

Ziiip.

She curled her fingers at the waistband of his boxer briefs, ready to expose his hard-on, but he batted her hands away. "I didn't say you could touch me. Hands at your back." He cast a meaningful look in my direction, one Katherine didn't miss, and it became clear that this had nothing to do with her.

This was all about me.

He pulled his cock out and aimed the tip at her willing mouth. "Do you want to suck me off?" he asked her.

"Yes."

"Yes *what?*"

"Yes, Mr. Channing."

"Do you want me to fuck you?"

"Please, Mr. Channing."

He leaned forward and almost brushed her lips with his cock, but his words were for me. "Capture this picture, Kayla. Keep it at the forefront of your mind. If you *ever* touch another man again, I'll not only fuck her, but I'll do it in front of you."

Katherine studied him, a brewing storm shadowing her features as realization dawned. But he was too busy watching for my reaction to notice. Too busy shooting a promise of dark truth from his eyes.

"I'll fuck her for hours. She'll take my cock in her cunt, in her ass, in her damn mouth. I'll make her scream my name for as long as it takes until the thought of *looking* at another man makes you sick."

I detected no bullshit in his tone. No bluffing. The warning was real. Set in stone. He'd laid down the law. For the rest of my life, if I stepped out of line again, he held the power to hit me where it would hurt the most…just like I'd hit his bullseye.

Silence descended upon the three of us. Gage drew in a breath as he zipped his pants.

"You're free to go," he told Katherine.

"But—"

"That will be all. You know where the door is."

Hell, if that bitch didn't look disappointed as she left us alone in the basement.

22. COMMON GROUND

The two of us were like oil and water, fire and ice. Love and Hate. None of those things mixed, but Gage and I were drawn to each other, nevertheless. Apart, we straddled the border of sane, but together we were a nuclear meltdown waiting to happen. Toxic chemicals emitting fatal fumes.

None of that mattered when we were in bed because our compatibility in that single, intense place overrode the incompatibilities.

Katherine's presence in the midst of our chaos was but a faint memory as his arms sheltered me, enclosed me in his possessive embrace. We sat in the middle of the bed, naked, the sheets a puddle around our joined bodies. Moans rent the air between frantic kisses. I clung to his sweat-slicked chest, my cheek on his shoulder as I rode him.

"Baby, yes." His strong hands gripped my hips, jerking me onto his cock in forceful plunges. "Fuck yes." He groaned. "Take me deep."

We came together at regular intervals. Up. Down. Up. Down.

Steady.

Sensual.

Sex in its basest form, yet what we were doing eclipsed fucking. We were crashing into each other in a wave of forgiveness, of absolution.

I cried out, just a few strokes away from creaming all over him. "Gage, please…oh God, please. I need to come." I panted, teeth pulling on my lower lip.

"You don't have permission."

"Please…please…can't hold back. Begging you…" I clawed at his shoulders, about to climb out of my skin and burrow into his.

He brought me down on his cock hard and held me there. "Look at me, baby."

I veered back, my breath coming fast between parted lips, and met his gaze—his heated, seductive gaze that pulled me into the depths of intense blue. I could lose myself forever in those eyes. In his arms. In the joining of our bodies.

Forever didn't seem long enough.

"Do I have your whole heart?" he asked, watching me closely.

"It beats for only you."

"Do I own this body?"

"Always."

"Am I yours?"

"I hope so." I leaned forward and caught his mouth, taking what I needed. Hoping he'd give it to me.

And he did. He thrust his tongue into my mouth and moaned in a way that made me whimper. Low and deep in his throat. The taste of him sent me reeling.

"I need you," I whispered against his lips.

He expelled a shaky breath. "You have me. Nothing and no one is taking you from me, or I from you." He ran a thumb over my lower lip. "Do you have something you need to ask me?"

Only every day for the rest of my life. "Will you forgive me?"

He pushed my damp bangs back and kissed my forehead. "You taught me about forgiveness, Kayla. You showed me what it meant to be forgiven. Because of your grace and heart, I learned to love. Baby, you were forgiven before you ever committed the crime."

I kissed him again, tears flooding my eyes. Joy grabbing hold of my soul. "I love you, Gage."

"Who am I, Kayla?"

"My Master."

Always.

Kayla Sutton has finally submitted.

And now that Gage has his wife under his control again, he won't stop until he's extracted every last independent drop from her being.

As each day passes, she learns new ways to accept his dominion. After all, she has a lot to atone for. Flirting with disaster with her ex-lover turned brother-in-law might be forgivable, but it's not so easily forgotten.

And neither are skeletons. If there's one thing Kayla has learned it's that skeletons don't just come out of the closet— they bust through with the power of a locomotive, mindless of the destruction they cause.

For the sake of her sanity, Kayla must make a tough decision, even if it means leaving the only man who's ever owned her, heart and soul.

Please visit my website to find where you can purchase The Devil's Wife: www.authorgemmajames.com/books

Acknowledgments

Since publishing for the first time in 2012, I've learned how awesome readers and bloggers are. I've learned how supportive my fellow authors are. I've met many people on this dark journey, both online and in person, and I'm beyond grateful to know each and every one of you. I'm bringing up the journey rather than the short side trip I took with this book because The Devil's Kiss Series started it all. Looking back, I'm in awe that a 12,000 word novelette snowballed into a series with twists and turns even I didn't see coming. More amazing is how it sparked to life a career I had only dreamed about.

So, to my fans, there are no words to express how thankful I am that you not only found me, but that you liked my books enough to come back for more. Your messages, emails, and comments have made me laugh and cry because you've touched me that much. So thank you, a million times thank you for giving me the chance to live my dream.

I'd also like to shout out to a few ladies who either took the time to read parts of The Devil's Wife, or helped me in other ways: Rachel, Kashunna, and Momo—thanks for your feedback and enthusiasm for this story. And to Deb: you are AWESOME. Thank you, ladies, for all you do. If you've followed my blog, joined my newsletter, liked me on Facebook, joined my Naughty Nook group, or followed me anywhere else, I owe you a big thank-you and a hug as well. Last but not least, Linda from Sassy Savvy Fabulous rocks. I've got to give you props for tolerating my brand of crazy. And speaking of people that rock, Kylie from Give Me Books is spectacular in that area too. I'm thrilled I got to meet you in person.

About the Author

Gemma James is a USA Today bestselling author of a blend of genres, from new adult contemporary to dark romance. She loves to explore the darker side of human nature in her fiction, and she's morbidly curious about anything dark and edgy, from deviant sex to serial killers. Readers have described her stories as being "not for the faint of heart."

She warns you to heed their words! Her playground isn't full of rainbows and kittens, though she likes both. She lives in middle-of-nowhere Oregon with her husband, two children, and a gaggle of animals.

For more information on available titles, please visit www.authorgemmajames.com

Made in the USA
Las Vegas, NV
21 December 2023